THE CITY OF FACTORIES

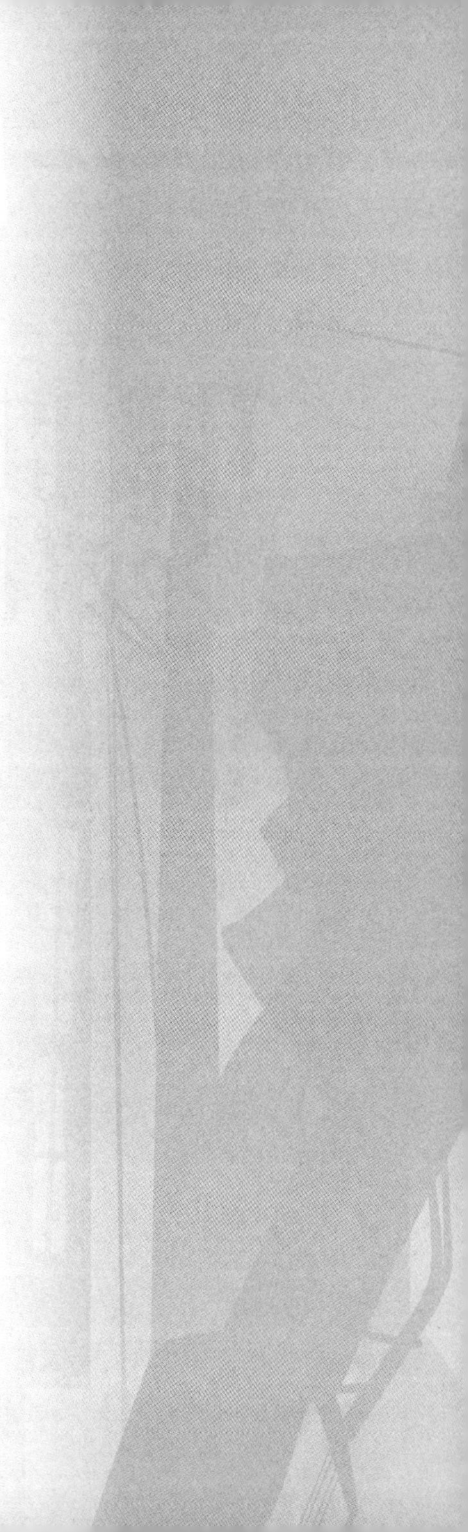

THE CITY OF FACTORIES

NAOMI ESELOJOR

RUADÁN
BOOKS

BOSTON, MA

The City of Factories

ISBN 978-1-968143-20-6 (trade paperback)
ISBN 978-1-968143-21-3 (ebook)
ISBN 978-1-968143-22-0 (audiobook)
Library of Congress Control Number: 2026937374

Edited by R. B. Wood
Cover Illustration by Sharif Muhammad
Design / Formatting by Leah Donell

First Edition

RUADÁN
BOOKS

RuadanBooks.com

For my younger self,
who never stopped believing.

1

APRIL 11, 1866
ITU AGAN VILLAGE, SNAKE ISLAND

Alabi stuffed his sack with a coarse wrapper, a hand-drawn map, a dagger, and a handful of fruit. At the bottom of his sack, he carefully tucked away a pair of binoculars of his own creation. He fingered his travel permit, a copper badge that glistened like a spark under the intrusive sunlight. With his eyes pressed shut, he held the cool metal close to his chest, relishing the weight of it. For several months, this badge had been his singular focus; now, at eighteen, it was the only ray of hope his family had left.

Even as the struggle to acquire the travel permit took two years out of the eighteen years of his life, he considered it a solitary ray of hope for his family. Because of it, Alabi had the opportunity to leave his village and gain entry to the industrial complex of the City of Factories—a promise of passage without the sting of persecution. When he put the travel permit close to his face, he could hear the faint, metallic tick-tock sounds of its internal timer. Two months of freedom. That was all the automaton government would give.

Alabi shared the achievement with Labake, his mother, who sobbed softly when she saw the travel permit. She ran her trembling fingers over Alabi's bare chest, tracing the protruding scars and ragged bumps on his mocha-brown skin.

Hours passed, and Alabi watched his shrivelled mother from the shadows of the passageway. Her favourite spot to think was on a large stone at the front of their home. She had just recovered from malaria, so she had been more quiet than usual. Since knowing that Alabi would soon leave, she'd been ruminating, her hollow eyes fixed on a soot-stained platoon of automaton soldiers patrolling the village. Alabi worried for her as she was ageing far too quickly. Even he knew it was not old age that left his mother wrinkled and grey. It all began nine years ago when the automatons invaded. Alabi remembered it with terrifying clarity as if it were yesterday.

Rays of sunlight rested on the rippling blue sea where a group of fishermen launched their nets. On the shores were a handful of villagers—women with wicker baskets, tightening their faded wrappers and gossiping as they anticipated a glorious catch. Little children ran across the sand, occasionally reprimanded by Elder Digiola's stern eyes and her gnarled walking stick, which also served as a rod of discipline.

Nine-year-old Alabi sat by the cavern of boats and watched Korede, his father, adjust the intricate metal parts of his new steam-powered prototype. The steamboat was what he called it, and unlike his common canoe, it was twelve inches long, cast from sturdy copper, and fitted with two wooden propellers for easy navigation.

Alabi watched as his father started the boat's engine and placed the trembling vessel onto the water. The prototype huffed, dispensing jittery wafts of white smoke as it drifted on the choppy sea waves. Korede watched the prototype go with triumph in his eyes. "It worked!" he said to Alabi, who had learnt to mimic his father's excitement despite having no clue why that mechanical breakthrough was important. Alabi jumped and squealed, but his eyes soon took on a worried expression. "Look, Bàámì," he said, "the steamboat will get lost at sea."

"You're right," Korede said, patting his son's head before shoving a canoe towards the water. Heads turned towards Korede as he paddled after his machine with practised grace, exchanging a smile with his friend Muees, who steadied a nearby vessel.

Alabi watched his father go with pride. Among the other men at sea, Korede was the bulkiest. His broad, sculpted frame, slick with sweat, was a spectacle Alabi considered glorious. Korede was one of the most respected men in the village, known for his exceptional fishing skills and his extraordinary inventions. After all, he had built brass engines that could tap water from the ground, along with steam-powered ploughs and excavators for the plantation farmers.

Suddenly, a colossal shadow blocked the sun and Alabi looked up. He squinted, angled his head as he tried to decipher what it was. That was not a cloud, but a hundred-foot dirigible bearing the golden insignia of a crown. "Bàámì, look up!" Alabi said.

He watched the dirigible hover, marvelling at the ribbed intricacy of the curved frame and hisses of vapour ejecting from the massive metallic engines. The fishermen gasped and murmured in dismay as they paddled their canoes in a hasty retreat.

"Alabi, run to your mother!" his father bellowed.

Alabi hesitated. The airship was lowering itself with a heavy groan, as if it were preparing to land on their island.

"Go, I'll be right behind you," his father insisted.

Alabi nodded and scampered through the village, hurrying past a group of elders having a meeting, and women weaving vibrant aṣọ òkè fabrics, all of them watching the sky with their mouths agape. He spotted his mother and ran to meet her.

"Bàámì is still out there," Alabi reported, but Labake's eyes were fixed on the sky, even as she caught him in her arms.

The flying object manoeuvred over trees and hamlets,

shearing the roofs from the gángan drummer's house and the village shrine as it passed. The men in the village grabbed their cutlasses, spears, and charms while the women cut and brandished large sticks as they held onto their children. Chaos broke loose as the market women abandoned their baskets of produce. The elders under the meeting tree cowered in fear, their voices rising as they called out to the gods of the land. Men, women, and children scattered across the village, ducking, screaming, trying to escape the looming dirigible that was now hovering only a few metres away. Amidst the pandemonium, Alabi sighted his father ushering the villagers to safety.

"Korede!" Labake cried with relief. Korede hurried towards them and scooped his wife and son in a tight embrace. By then, the dirigible had landed at the village square, its monstrous size filling the entire space.

The vessel hissed open and scores of automaton soldiers marched out with a heavy, synchronized thud. Until then, Alabi hadn't thought anything was bigger than his father. His father was hefty, but the automatons were hulking and unyielding. They were taller than most and shaped like humanoid beings of cold, riveted metal. Steam hissed from the exposed tubes in their backs as they held shiny weapons of fine wood and brass.

Scanning through the crowd, the biggest of them asked, "Where is the village chief?"

The people watched in stupefaction as the metal figure

spoke in an imprecise, rattling mimicry of the Yoruba language. Atobatele, the commander of the Itu Agan army, stepped forward, fixing malevolent eyes on the automaton. He held his sharpened cutlass in his right hand, a cluster of powerful protective charms on display. A group of warriors followed his lead, advancing towards the metal soldiers, waiting for their commander's signal to attack.

"Why do you want our chief?" Atobatele asked.

A minute seemed like an eternity until the automaton spoke. "Surrender him or die."

There was a collective gasp. Alabi's mother pulled him a few steps back, trembling for their safety. Korede remained in his spot, fists clenched. He was a man, and so he could not run. Atobatele lunged at the automaton, his cutlass sparking as it sliced across its chest. The other warriors acted in unison, each of them engaging an automaton in a sudden, frantic battle. Alabi couldn't see much of what happened after the engagement began, but he heard screams, the sickening ripping of metal tearing through flesh, and the piercing cries of Atobatele's wife and child. Alabi froze in horror when he realised what had happened. He couldn't believe it: Atobatele's charms, which were supposed to protect him—protect their community—had failed.

The remaining automatons cocked their weapons and fired at the village warriors, felling them with bullets to their chests. The corpses of the warriors splayed on top of each other in a pile, blood seeping from their grievous wounds. The automatons, on the other hand, were left without a single dent on their reinforced brass armour.

Once again, the automatons asked, "Where is the village chief?"

The people pressed their hands against their mouths in an attempt to contain their shock. Even Atobatele's wife stifled her whimpers as the village chief—old, grey, and adorned in traditional clay beads—shuffled out. Holding his white horsetail with trembling fingers, he walked through a parted huddle of desolate villagers. An ominous silence rested on the village as the chief cowered before the automatons.

"Please," he begged, tears furrowing down his cheeks. "Don't kill any more of us."

"We won't if you cooperate," the automaton said, and a brief exchange ensued. The chief's eyes grew paler and paler with each passing second, the cold, calculating destruction of the invaders draining the very life from his face.

"Spare him!" a voice cried from the huddle of villagers. It was Elder Digiola, her rod of discipline forgotten in the dust as she reached out a withered hand. "He has done nothing but protect our village!"

The Chief looked at his people, his white horsetail trailing in the dirt and mud under the oppressive grip of the machine that held him.

"Do not beg, Digiola," he rasped, his voice a dry whisper against the automaton's metallic hum. "My duty is to my people, and I am willing to sacrifice myself so no one else does."

"Is there no price?" Muees shouted, stepping forward beside the other fishermen. "Take our catch! Take our land! Just leave us our father!"

The automaton didn't turn its head; it simply adjusted its stance, the gears in its neck clicking with cold indifference.

By the end of their discussion, they forced the chief to his knees in the blood-soaked dirt.

"We are to execute you by the order of the Queen Mother," the automaton said, pointing its long-barrelled weapon between the eyes of the helpless chief.

"Wait!" someone shouted near Alabi. He looked to see his teary-eyed father panting heavily. Beads of sweat trickled down his forehead. "Don't kill him, please," Korede said, the tiny copper steamboat still clutched in his grasp.

The automaton tilted its head to the side and stared at Alabi's father through vacant jet-black screens where eyes should have been. Without a flicker of hesitation, there was a loud bang and the chief lay motionless on the dusty ground, blood pooling from his forehead. A man beside Alabi white-knuckled his cutlass in readiness to attack, but Korede motioned to him with a sharp, frantic gesture to stay his fury. The automaton walked across the corpse without hesitation, approaching Korede with slow, intimidating strides. Korede pushed himself forward, a desperate move to lead the automatons away from the people, away from his wife and son.

As Korede got closer, the automatons didn't attack him. *Why didn't they attack?* Alabi wondered, his heart hammering against his ribs.

Labake choked back tears. She held onto Alabi, her fingers digging deep into his skin like iron clamps. More automatons marched out of the dirigible, arranging themselves in precise twos and ordering the villagers to split themselves into groups. The air filled with the abrasive sound of grinding gears and harsh commands as the machines forcibly arranged everyone. One group would include men and the other, women and children.

Alabi latched onto his mother, grateful that he wouldn't be separated from her. He craned his neck in search of his father but didn't get a good view through the forest of metal limbs. It wasn't until Alabi's mother tugged at him that he realised they had started to move. The women and children, accompanied by a troop of metal men, walked to a spot under a mango tree. By the time Alabi and his mother returned to the village centre, the airship and his father were gone.

Recently, several weary travellers had confirmed that Korede, along with the finest craftsmen in the land, was being forced to work for the regime in the sprawling factory in Apapa.

Alabi swung the sack over his shoulders, walked towards his mother, and tenderly squeezed her shoulders. For the next two months, Alabi's mother would become human collateral, destined to be taken by the automatons if he didn't return before his permit expired. The thought of something bad happening to her made his chest ache with a dull, throbbing pressure, but they had both admitted that they needed this closure.

Alabi leaned beside her ear and whispered, "I'm ready to leave."

Labake stared at her son for a moment. "Promise me you will return," she said, lips trembling as tears spilled from her eyes. Alabi couldn't bear to see his mother cry. He pulled her in for a tight embrace and allowed himself to bask in her familiar, homely scent. She'd always smelled like the kitchen—a comforting blend of onions, earthy leaves, and spice. Her hugs, warm and enriching, filled his soul with vitality. Even when he returned home from work exhausted and battered, even when he grieved the absence of his father, she had always been there to comfort him.

Alabi pulled away from his mother, tears flowing down his cheeks as he gently cupped her face. "Nothing will happen to us," Alabi said, wiping her face with his thumb.

"I swear to you that I will return. I will find my father, and I will bring him home."

2

APRIL, 12, 1866
APAPA, EKO COLONY
THE CITY OF FACTORIES

Alabi straightened himself as soon as the checkpoint came into view. A boat had preceded him to the Apapa docks, and the occupants were waiting to present their travel permits and to have their belongings rifled through. Alabi couldn't make out the exact number of automatons in the semi-darkness of the morning, but he could see the predatory glint of their metallic frames and the unyielding yellowish-orange light emitting from their eyes. Alabi, tired of witnessing the routine mistreatment of his people, prayed that the men on the boats had nothing incriminating that would get them accosted, or worse. The automatons mostly confiscated weapons, bars of gold from miners, cowries, and rare minerals. They were also fond of seizing foodstuffs to maintain a stranglehold on their distribution. It was for this reason that Alabi's mother nurtured a secret garden in their living room where she grew her own yams and vegetables.

While Alabi waited to be searched, the sun bloomed

over the horizon, casting light on what had been the looming silhouette of the great city of Apapa. He'd heard many stories about the City of Factories—of the mind-bending inventions and labyrinthine structures. It was just the type of place his father would thrive in, if he weren't being treated like a slave in his own country. Muees had sworn by the gods that he had seen Korede when he went to the city two years ago. He said the encounter was brief, but he was sure it was him.

"He had changed," Muees had said with a deep sigh. "I wonder what they've done to him."

Alabi paddled forward so the automatons could probe his boat. He had prepared for this search and created a hidden compartment within the hull where he hid his dagger, his food, and his map. The automatons flashed their glowing eyes first at the travel permit, then on the bilge where they scoured through Alabi's sack with a massive magnet. They also made sure Alabi took his clothes off and turned his pockets inside out. In the end, the metal men motioned rigidly for him to pass and Alabi rowed away. Even as he was free to go, he could feel the smouldering heat of their glowing eyes as they bored into his back.

Years ago, Alabi's father used to travel to Apapa to buy supplies, and upon his return, told tales of the busy market stalls and gigantic cargo ships conveying goods and white men in cotton shirts. Since the advent of the automatons, there had been a significant decrease in the presence of these white slavers. What the country had instead were wealthy, brown-skinned noblemen called the Zul, who draped themselves in fine leathers. They considered the automaton government business partners and were responsible for funding most of their projects in exchange for advanced technology and bondservants. This wealthy minority, despite being allied with of the Queen Mother, was hardly ever seen on the common streets, except in ornate carriages guarded by imposing armoured automaton soldiers.

After paying the docking fee for his boat, Alabi walked past soot-stained spherical and rectangular structures of iron and brickwork—an array of small, medium, and massive buildings, each possessing tall cylindrical chimneys spewing plumes of charcoal-grey smoke. From the large-paned windows, Alabi spotted workers performing meticulous tasks under the watchful glow of mechanical eyes. Nearly every structure hummed with the vibration of rotating cogs and was sealed by heavy, riveted iron doors. Alabi viewed the intricate architecture as a double-edged sword; it not only showed the stifled creativity of Apapa's artisans but also the extent of the automaton government's wealth. It worried him that they grew more formidable while his people suffered.

Alabi's senses were quickly overwhelmed by the bitter scent of chemicals, the rhythmic hiss of steam, and the distant, laboured snarls and grunts of factory workers. Above it all rose the cacophony of the city: the clicking, ticking, grating, and roaring of clockwork engines, punctuated by the strident clang of metal against metal. Automaton soldiers patrolled the streets, standing at the corners like iron sentinels and apprehending anyone they deemed suspicious. They'd caught a homeless child and were detaining her when a sudden tremor shook the ground.

An ear-splitting boom tore through the air, followed by thick billows of black smoke clawing into the sky. The earth trembled as shards of glass rained down from splintered windows. Dazed by what he had just witnessed, Alabi pulled himself into a ducking position and scrambled to hide under a nearby cart. The automaton soldiers, scattered throughout the city at various checkpoints, paused their obligations momentarily, before turning sharply towards the explosion in unnerving simultaneity. Their eyes glowed a menacing red as they drew their weapons and disappeared into the smoky haze. Alabi had no doubt in his mind that it was the Orah resistance.

There was a burst of colourful smoke as a blur of respirator-wearing raiders invaded a workshop and loaded their sacks with supplies and gadgets. They were quick—noiseless—and ghost-like; Alabi could only spot glimpses of them—obfuscated forms moving swiftly in a coordinated fashion—because he peeked from beneath his hiding place. Automaton reinforcements thundered into the plaza, making their way into the smoky haze with heavy, rhythmic stomps. Alabi had not seen so many of them in one place since the invasion. There had to be twenty at least. Even with their numbers, Alabi could hear the resistance team scamper away with a jingly sack of equipment. They had escaped.

Hunkered down behind some crates, Alabi waited until evening, when the smoke had cleared, and the thunderous footsteps of automaton soldiers had become distant. Workers pooled out of the factories in hundreds, their faces coloured with sweat and soot, mask-like with exhaustion. Alabi slipped into the throng of people, the crowd being ushered into their work quarters by patrol automatons. He scanned the sea of faces for his father as he walked the path that he had committed to memory from his map. Because Alabi held a travel permit, he couldn't reside with the bonded workers of Apapa. Instead, he made his way to a smaller housing facility.

Muees mentioned that it was south-east of the city, adjacent to the workers' quarters. It had been a shack the last time he visited and remained a shack by the time Alabi walked in. The front door creaked on rusted hinges as it swung open, and Alabi was relieved to find two other men sitting on one of the three bunk beds available in the room. He lowered his sack on one of the beds and greeted his new roommates. Regardless of where Alabi stepped, the rotting wood of the old shack groaned. Mice and cockroaches hurried past him, crawling over his feet with a bold indifference as if he were some fixture or merely another piece of the decaying furniture.

"First time?" a man with a raspy voice asked. Alabi couldn't help but notice his sharp, pronounced jaw and the jagged texture of his patched brows.

Alabi nodded. "And you?"

"I've been here a few times, Biodun too. I am Ige, by the way." He offered a hand in greeting. "We're both from Eti-Osa and came to transport fish from our hometown to the city. What about you? Where'd you come from?"

"I'm Alabi from Itu Agan," Alabi said, reflexively extending his palms to catch a sack of food that Biodun tossed his way. He opened the sack and sniffed it skeptically. Deciding it was safe, he inhaled the yeasty aroma before stuffing his face with the morsel of bread inside.

"You are not entitled to a free meal with your travel permit, but I figured you'd be hungry," Biodun said. "Of course, if you want more of that, you could let me know. We can help you smuggle food for a fair deal. They accept just about anything over here: clothes, food, scraps—even people," Ige said with a dark, rattling laugh, and Biodun elbowed him hard. "You never told us what you are here for."

Alabi swallowed his food and, for an instant, felt a spark of power surge within him. His eyes widened with grim clarity. "I am here to find my father."

There was a heavy minute of silence as Ige and Biodun

exchanged guarded looks. "Was your father taken?" Biodun asked.

"Nine years ago, yes," Alabi answered, nodding, "but someone from my village found him here recently. He is rumoured to be working for the regime, in one of those factories that build heavy machinery."

"There are not many of those factories in the city, so you don't need to look too hard," Ige said, his voice dropping to a cautious whisper. "However, even if you do find these factories, your travel permit doesn't grant you access to places like that, especially the top-secret ones shrouded by heightened security. Your best bet to explore the city would be to do it undercover—and even that can cost you your life."

"I would advise you to think this through," Biodun added solemnly. "Nine years is a long time. You wouldn't want to risk your life over a rumour."

Alabi settled on the creaking bed and allowed himself a minute to ponder. He didn't come all the way to the city to give up on the first day, not when he had spent nearly every night for the past decade dreaming of seeing his father again.

"My father is alive," Alabi said, his voice hardening with a certainty that left no room for doubt. "He is a brilliant inventor, and he is in this city. I just need to know where to look."

Biodun was about to argue, but Ige squeezed his shoulder. "Would you be willing to risk your life for this cause?"

"I would do anything."

"You see, Alabi, we would love to help you, but nothing in this city comes free," Ige said, his eyes glinting with a tinge of merchant's greed—or was it merely hunger? Alabi wasn't sure if he could tell the difference. "Everything comes with a price." Alabi studied him for a moment before deciding to bite.

"How much?" Alabi asked with a sigh of resignation.

"Anything useful from that sack of yours."

Alabi scanned the contents in the sack, rating them by order of value and importance. Eventually, he presented his dagger to the smirking, bulgy-eyed Ige. Ige inspected the weapon with practised ease, checking for chips, scratches, and flaws in the steel. When he found none, Alabi took back his dagger for a final moment before letting it go.

"I would also want dinner in addition to what you want to tell me," Alabi said, refusing to be completely cheated.

Ige's eyes narrowed in suspicion, but seeing Alabi's resolve, he agreed. He patted Alabi on the shoulder and tossed the dagger into a sack brimming with mismatched collectibles.

Biodun and Ige exchanged looks, and upon a nod of approval, Biodun spoke:

"There are two ways you can find your father. One is to help capture an important member of the Orah resistance. The government rewards those who support the dictatorship with lavish cruelty. You could even come to own an apartment in the Government Reserved Areas, gain access to a better life and more freedom… but proving your loyalty to the automaton government could cost you your soul—and your life."

Alabi's lips trembled in disgust. He would rather be cut into a thousand pieces than join forces with the automaton government. "What is the second way?"

The men shared wary glances. Ige looked around, checked the windows and the shadowed threshold before returning inside. "You could join the Orah resistance," Ige whispered, his voice barely audible over the groaning of the shack. "They've been fighting this regime for years and have a solid whisper network, so they would know which factories to search—even, potentially, your father's whereabouts. I don't know where the resistance may be, but expect them in unexpected places: in factories, workshops, in the streets, on the rooftops. They also have spies everywhere."

Ige leaned in closer, his protuberant eyes reflecting the dim light. "My only advice to you is to be careful. They can be just as ruthless as the automaton government. If they discover you're out searching for them, they might not question your intentions; they might kill you before you can even speak your father's name."

Alabi had heard about the resistance and their fearless pursuit of independence. After seeing them in action earlier, he thought it was the bravest thing ever to challenge the government. Even as he admired them, though, he couldn't help but wonder if he was walking into a calculated deathtrap, and if these men—Ige and Biodun—could be trusted, or if they were merely setting him up for a fall.

At dawn, a loud metallic hum permeated the air, followed by the harsh crackling sound of conical speakers coming to life. Alabi jolted up, his heart pounding as he struggled to decipher the distorted sound.

"Attention, people of Apapa and visitors," the voice began with a flat, emotionless tone. "Yesterday, the resistance struck again, and the explosion claimed the lives of two strays."

The voice became colder, a rasp of static punctuating the words: "In accordance with the laws implemented by our supreme leader, the Queen Mother, let it be known that whosoever is caught in affiliation with the resistance will have to choose between a public execution and wasting away in our deepest dungeons. This is your only warning.

"To those who remain loyal to our cause, any information leading to the arrest of the resistance members will be rewarded with a golden badge and a home in the Government Reserved Areas with our esteemed partners, the

Zul. Do remember that automaton soldiers still patrol the streets and might stop you to demand a means of identification. If you are at your duty posts or you can prove you are not in alliance with the resistance, our automatons will spare you. Do not forget to remain obedient to our government and to shun treason. Long live the Queen."

The message ended with a piercing static hiss and then nothing. A heavy, suffocating silence followed the end of the speech.

"Two strays died?" Alabi asked in a mumble.

"That's what they said," Ige said, his voice thick with sleep. "My advice: don't always believe everything they announce. The automaton government is fond of exaggerating the number of deaths and systematically villainising the resistance."

Alabi wasn't convinced, and Ige seemed determined to persuade him. He assumed a sitting position, a glistening streak of saliva connecting the corner of his lips to his jaw.

"The factory the Orahs destroyed was an aether-fuel plant, a pulsing heart of plasma and lightning used as an alternative source of energy for airships and automatons. For years, the toxic smoke from the plant has been the leading cause of lung infections, breathing problems, and even death. Whenever a worker in the city gets sick, the automaton government quickly looks for a replacement. It is like changing the worn wheels of a cart. Why fix it when you have many others to choose from? The only problem is that people aren't wheels. They're humans, and their lives should be valuable."

Ige leaned forward, his gaze intensifying. "The resistance did what they had to do to save the majority, Alabi. So what if a couple of people die in the process? In a world like ours, there is no room for sentiment. It is either kill or be killed."

Alabi's stomach rumbled, and a knowing smile crept onto Ige's face. "You know, you could trade more stuff for a free meal," he teased.

Alabi kissed his teeth in annoyance and strode out the door with his sack fitted tightly on his back. The sun had risen, but the streets were eerie and void of people; mostly because their shifts were yet to begin and they were wary of breaking curfew. Alabi took out his map and studied it. His father was spotted at one of the factories at the heart of the city, where armoured automatons patrolled in menacing multitudes. Even with the travel permit, it would be dangerous for him to visit that area alone, especially without any type of protection and a concrete plan of action.

Alabi compared the map to the actual city, and realised with a sinking heart that there were many changes. The government had built new steel mills, warehouses, and even a cavernous airship hangar; old paths led to new places, and new structures seemed to be getting renovated before the mortar even dried. Alabi looked around at the sprawling industrial landscape and caught a glimpse of an old hut crammed between two workshops. It was a crumbling relic spared from the iron tide—a trace of an old world. A world without automatons.

Alabi headed west and was turning a corner when he bumped into a scrawny teenager.

"Oh! Pardon me," the boy said, his eyes fixed on the floor as he held a threadbare blanket clinging to his shoulders. Alabi got a pungent whiff of tobacco and palm wine when the stray spoke, but he overlooked it since the boy appeared harmless.

A few steps later, Alabi realised his sack had been stolen. He whipped around just in time to glimpse the fluttering hem of the boy's blanket before he shifted into an alley. Alabi hurried after him, swerving towards the alley with mounting caution. The teenager, thankfully, was still in sight, his gait unsteady like he was being tossed about by an invisible hand. Alabi surveyed the area. He had no weapon and little knowledge of the city's layout so he had to be calculative. If an automaton caught him tackling a boy, he could be sanctioned for violence.

He began walking hurriedly and, when he was sure the coast was clear, broke into a sprint. He had almost reached his target when the boy spun around, glaring at Alabi with shimmering golden eyes. Alabi instantly sensed a strange force, but by then, it was too late.

He stiffened, forehead creased in confusion as he felt every muscle in his body go limp and slack. The stray landed a swift kick to Alabi's gut, and he found himself plunging face-first into the gritty ground. The thief took off his blanket, revealing a complex array of charms on his chest and arms that seemed to hum with the same strange energy as his eyes. He set Alabi's sack on his back, considered him for a moment as if admiring the damage he had done, and tottered away.

It took about five hours for the paralysis to completely wear off. During that time, the city had come alive and a cacophony of discordant sounds filled the air. Automaton patrols nearly trampled Alabi as they strode heavily through, scouting the streets with rhythmic, unfeeling steps. Factory workers sidestepped past him, their worn slippers splattering mud and debris all over his paralysed body.

A couple of raggedy little girls appeared beside Alabi and began frisking his pockets for anything saleable. Rays of the morning sun bounced off the travel permit, causing the girls to consider it with bright, desperate eyes.

Alabi internally writhed with displeasure, just able to raise his head to see the faces of the children who were stealing from him. Tears filled his eyes as he tried to speak, tried to plead with them not to take his travel permit. The rest he could replace. He could find another map; he could build different binoculars, but he couldn't afford to lose his badge. Alabi could only let out a low moan, but even then, the girls didn't stop. They lifted the travel permit and regarded it with innocent wonder. They passed it one to another and took turns listening to the delicate clicking sound of the timer. Giggles of delight broke from their lips as the tallest of them slid it in her pocket and they scampered away.

Alabi stumbled on a reflection of himself in one of the giant windows. A few more days and he would look like a stray, indistinguishable from the strange boy with the blanket. It was his second day in the city, and he had been stripped bare, left with nothing but his burning resolve. Alabi had long underestimated the power of charms, especially since they seemed useless against the cold iron of the automatons. Then again, he had never been attacked with magic before. Back home, even after the invasion, he didn't have strangers preying on him and trying to rob him of his belongings. They were a small, close-knit village where everyone knew everyone and considered themselves family. They didn't have half the resources of a major city, but at least they considered the automaton government a common enemy.

It was different in Apapa, which had a desperate number of strays. Here even the children had lost their innocence. The weak were threatened by people and automatons alike, and not many saw humanity in the next person. They saw commodities instead. *They accept just about anything over here: clothes, food, gadgets—even people,* Ige had said. *Even people,* Alabi echoed internally, the words an ominous punctuation.

As he made his way to the explosion site, he became hyper-aware of his surroundings and raised his fist in a shaky defence whenever he heard footsteps approaching. Alabi noticed himself gradually drifting into hysteria and took a break to arrange his thoughts and steady his racing heart. The journey still stretched on far ahead, and he couldn't afford to lose himself so soon. Even as his legs weakened and his stomach growled—even as his breathing came in ragged bursts and the sun scorched his back—he was determined to keep going.

Without his travel permit, he could no longer walk around boldly, so he stuck to the shadows like a cockroach, advancing only when the coast was clear, and sticking to the paths he partially recognised. He had the much safer choice of returning to the shack, but since he was on a time limit, he couldn't afford to waste an entire day. Alabi kept an eye out for the children who had stolen from him, hoping that before the end of the day, he would somehow get his stuff back.

The explosion site was heavily guarded by automaton soldiers. In spite of the distance between the site and his hiding spot, Alabi could make out a medium-sized crater, a jagged wound in the earth surrounded by flecks of glass and debris where the blast had occurred. He scanned the adjoining buildings for any sign of the resistance, trying to make out figures amidst the shimmering, sweltering heat. It was for this reason he had built his binoculars, and now he had lost them. An aching pain in his belly resurfaced, reminding him of the boy's kick earlier in the day. That, coupled with his roaring stomach and encroaching dizziness, made it harder for him to make out objects in the distance.

As much as Alabi wanted to achieve something that day, he felt inclined to respond to his body—to his parched throat and his wobbly legs. He could wait under the sun, attempt to manoeuvre through armoured automatons and scout for resistance members, or he could return to the shack, gather his strength, and properly plan his next course of action.

Alabi resorted to the latter plan and was about to leave when he spotted a hooded figure on the rooftop. A jolt of hope surged through him, but it was short-lived, as the silhouette vanished within seconds and Alabi was once again left to ponder his hollow life choices.

Ige and Biodun barely recognised Alabi when he showed up in the shack with filth-stained clothes and muddy hair.

"It's me, Alabi," he said in almost a whisper. At the mention of Alabi's name, their features softened and they burst into unfiltered, belly-aching laughter. They didn't ask him any questions, and Alabi was thankful that they didn't pry. Rather, Biodun tossed him half a loaf of bread and a gourd of water, which Alabi devoured within seconds like a starving animal.

Alabi fell on his bed, landing splayed, a puppet whose strings had been severed. The food and water brought him temporary relief, but it wasn't enough to completely quench his ravaging hunger. His stomach rumbled again. He needed more.

"This new regime has turned even the little ones into plunderers," Biodun said, and it dawned on Alabi that perhaps his misfortune wasn't unique.

"Do you know who it might be and where I can find the thieves?" Alabi asked.

"There're too many of them to identify," Ige said, shaking his head slowly. "Sorry, Alabi."

"I remember when we were little, Biodun," Ige said with a sudden childish longing. "When we had an abundance of food, all we did was play *boju-boju* and follow our parents to their farms. My father had acres of land back then and a thriving fishing business. He would take me with him and show me his massive plantation. My twelve brothers and I were to inherit it when he passed away."

Ige sighed, and a heavy silence fell on the shack. Alabi knew what it was like to live in the past, to savour the memories of a life that could have been. Now he'd faced an introduction to the brutal harshness of life in the city, of a culturally different and unforgiving terrain. It wouldn't take long before he, too, began to steal.

3

Wind tugged at the corrugated iron roofs of the old shack, causing the metal to patter in a syncopated rhythm. A cool breeze brought in drizzling rain, and soon, all three men stirred awake. They took out their gourds and water pots and placed them under the densely pouring rain. Dark clouds smothered the sky, leaving only a small opening for moonlight to seep through. Alabi wallowed in the rain. It was the first bath he had taken in days, a temporary escape from the torrid, stifling Èkó heat. He opened his mouth so the water could drop in and heaved a sigh of deep relief as the pleasing coolness eased his parched throat. He had had an unsuccessful week, and all he wanted to do was languish in the earthy smell of the downpour.

Alabi had become acutely aware of the swelling number of strays in the city—the young, the disabled, and the elderly. Despite this, he hadn't seen the boy with the blanket or the pair of girls that had stolen his travel permit, and after days of searching, he was beginning to accept that he might never see them again. He acquired a new sack in which he began hoarding gadgets that he planned to trade for food. The ghostly clicks of his missing freedom permit haunted him in his sleep and every day he grew more conscious of how quickly time passed.

He would linger as he edged past the explosion site, but the hooded figure never returned. The last time he was there, the automatons had nearly arrested him. They approached him, tilting their heads with a mechanical whine as if trying to calculate if he was a stray or not. When classifying Alabi proved too difficult, they issued him a warning and turned their attention to something else.

Alabi found himself hoping for an explosion—for anything that could grant him a lead on the resistance. Unfortunately, there were no further incidents and he had found no hints. Once, he heard someone creeping beside him and hurried after the sound, only to find a wild dog hunting for food. Because he didn't make any headway with finding the resistance, Alabi began secretly asking workers throughout the city if they knew his father. He would wait until shift changes and as they flowed out of their workplaces, he would beckon to them. He had done this for three consecutive days but found nothing. If they knew a Korede, he was either dead, non-existent, or simply not his father.

The rain stopped in the early afternoon, so Alabi decided to take a light stroll. Suddenly, he stopped in his tracks. Up ahead, three girls were rummaging through an upturned cart. Recognizing two of them as the permit thieves, Alabi's heart skipped a beat. He scrambled out of sight and watched them from a corner as the girls sorted through the cart's wreckage. Alabi thought briefly about chasing them, and demanding his travel permit, but there were three of them and only one of him. He had seen desperate girls defend themselves by screaming, biting, and hurling objects at their enemies; he didn't wish to hurt them, nor did he wish to attract the wrong attention, so he proposed to himself that he remain patient. He would follow them instead.

Once they had filled their gowns with metal parts, they scampered away, their footsteps nimble and light with caution. Alabi followed the girls through a strange route, navigating stagnant potholes in foul-smelling alleys and avoiding elderly or crippled strays extending withered hands, begging for help. While winding through a back accessway, the littlest of the girls slipped in a puddle, and the remaining two lifted her up, hastily scraping the mud from her clothes before continuing their journey. The girls swerved and sprinted and crawled and slipped around corners, but Alabi remained on their trail.

One of them whipped around, but Alabi had hidden behind a massive steel pipe. Gusts of hissing steam wafted around Alabi's crouched form, thick enough that he could hardly be seen through the mist. An automaton's heavy footsteps startled the girls, and they quickly crawled into a small opening in a weathered cobblestone building.

By the time Alabi squeezed through the hole, the girls

had spotted him. They retreated slowly, the eldest of them brandishing a rusted steel rod at Alabi.

"Stay back," she said, her voice thin but defiant.

Alabi looked at the girls—at the littlest one trembling behind her big sister. He had barely arranged his thoughts when the tallest of them rushed towards him and tried to clobber him with the rod. Alabi dodged her attack and swiftly bound her wrists behind her back with a braid of gauged wire.

"I just want what you stole from me," Alabi said as he slowly released her.

"We didn't take anything from you," the eldest argued, though her eyes darted nervously toward the other two.

"Lies!" Alabi protested. "A few days ago, I was paralysed, and while I was on the ground, your sisters took my freedom permit."

"It could've been anyone," the eldest said, her tone firm despite Alabi's intimidatory stance.

"We… We don't have it anymore. We sold it to some man for a meal," the second oldest said, ignoring her sister. Her emerald eyes glistened with tears. "Please, don't kill us."

Alabi looked at the eldest, whose features softened into a look of weary defeat. He looked between the other two girls, then around the decrepit building—at the gaping ceiling choked with cobwebs and holes large enough for a grass cutter to run through. There was a pile of faeces nearby, surrounded by a frantic halo of buzzing flies. Their living conditions were much worse than the old shack.

"I'm not going to hurt you," Alabi said, but the girls didn't seem persuaded, even as he unbound the eldest.

He took out his sack from underneath his blouse and the girls took another defensive step back. The littlest one had started to cry, a quiet, hiccuping sound that echoed through the hollow room. Alabi dipped his hand inside, took out three mangoes, and shared them among them. The oldest collected the mangoes, her eyes wide in shock. They hesitated, the air thick with a mutual suspicion, probably wondering whether the fruit was laced with poison. Alabi assured them it was safe to eat by taking a bite out of his own portion. When they saw him swallow, they sank their teeth into their own with a desperate ferocity, eating as fast as they could.

"I'm not going to hurt you," Alabi repeated, crouching now to speak to them on their level. He was especially sensitive to the littlest one, who looked about four years old. "My name is Alabi, and I am a traveller. What you took from me is very important, and I cannot complete my mission without it."

"We are sorry about your stuff," the eldest said at last, her voice losing its jagged edge. "We did what we had to do to survive." She met Alabi's gaze with an old, weary stare. "Thank you for not attacking us, and for the food. My name is Imade."

Imade looked about thirteen years old. She was tall for

her age, with a sharp brown gaze and the quiet prowess of a natural-born leader. "My sisters are Leila and Fara," Imade said.

Although Imade called them sisters and Alabi had presumed as much, he didn't notice any resemblance. In fact, Leila looked like she was of a different race, with her loose curls and the pale freckles on her nose. The youngest, Fara, clung to the other two and would either nod or shake her head when asked a question.

"I need to know who you sold my travel permit to. Where can I find them?" Alabi said, his tone pleading rather than demanding.

"We sold it to Zaza. He wears a mask and owns a black market by the workers' quarters. For safety reasons, he operates only after the workers' shifts are over," Imade said. "I would take you to him, but it is becoming increasingly dangerous for us at night, and we only travel as a group so no one gets left behind."

Alabi nodded in understanding, his mind already mapping the route to the quarters. "Don't worry. I will find him myself." He took one more look at the girls, a silent promise of safety in his eyes, but as he was about to leave, Leila stopped him.

"Be careful with Zaza," she cautioned, her voice dropping to a terrified whisper. "Don't look into his eyes."

A soft yellowish glow emanated from the workers' quarters as a steam-powered generator wheezed and rattled on. Inside the building were hundreds of bunk beds, occupied by twice the number of men of all ages. The cloying stench of sweat and musk filled the place; the space between the beds was so narrow that the men could hardly turn without touching. Alabi had worked for the regime as both a farmer and a fisherman for years, but his time in Apapa opened his eyes to a yawning social hierarchy. The workers were given bigger buildings, but they weren't allowed to be too comfortable—just enough to keep them docile and diligent. Two square meals and a squeaky bed in a rat-infested building felt like luxury to the strays, and the government had folks craving the privilege of factory workers despite it being nothing more than a glorified form of suffering. Compared to the good old days, where every house owned a farm and food was in abundance, the people of Apapa—be it workers or street urchins—lived like slaves in their own country.

It wasn't hard to find Zaza. He still had the same blanket wrapped around him, only this time, he had a mask over his face, completely obscuring his eyes. Alabi's gut throbbed as he remembered Zaza's kick.

"Three strays sold you a travel permit a few days ago. Where is it?" Alabi demanded.

Zaza raised his head to consider Alabi. "You're crazy if you think I remember every sale that I make. Also, it is common sense to know that travellers are more likely to be interested in travel permits."

Alabi was stunned by his bluntness. He pressed on, nonetheless. "What about my other stuff that you stole from me? My map, my binoculars? Who did you sell those to?"

Zaza strode closer to Alabi, so that his mask almost grazed his sweaty face. "Unless you have something to trade, I suggest you return to where you came from." His voice was a low, vibrating hum. "Be wary of how you speak to me, traveller, as I could do unimaginable things to you."

Alabi wanted so badly to punch that mask off his face, but instead, he drew back into the warm light of the workers' quarters. He couldn't compete with a magician yet, but he would get his revenge. He swore it to himself.

"I will be leaving by the end of this week," Biodun said, motioning to his travel permit. "Ige is out foraging, but he'll be staying longer. In case you come back one day and you don't meet me here, just know that I wish you luck. You're a brave young man, Alabi. I really hope you find your father."

Alabi felt his heart leap with gratitude. He would miss Biodun's rough generosity.

"Thank you, Biodun. I wish you the very best. Have a safe trip," Alabi said.

To Alabi's chagrin, Imade and her sisters showed up at the shack and met him sitting at the doorstep, pondering his next move.

"We wanted to see how you were doing," Imade said, her gaze scanning his tired face. "Did you find your permit?"

Alabi breathed a sigh of weary fortitude. "No."

"We're sorry," Fara said. It was the first time Alabi had heard her speak; her voice was a tiny, melodic bell in the silence of the slums.

"We've been feeling guilty," Leila added, her lips twisting into a pout. "Is there anything we can do to make up for it?"

"I think so." Alabi entered the shack and motioned to the girls to do the same. He shut the door, forcing it closed as far as the rusted hinges allowed, and began in a low, conspiratorial tone: "I've been looking for the Orah resistance group. Do you know where I can find them?"

"What do you want with them?" Imade asked, her brows creasing with alarm. "They're militants."

"I need their help to find my father. He's the reason I'm in this city. Please let me know if you've heard anything. It has been three weeks since my arrival, and I haven't made any progress. Please..."

It was Imade's turn to look around with hunted caution. She pulled her sisters closer and said, "We've seen the resistance members many times, gliding over the roofs wearing dark hoods and brass ventilators."

"Do you know where they are now?" Alabi questioned, with eyes so wide they could pop out of their sockets. His heart pounded against his ribs as he leaned forward.

"No," Leila said. "But I overheard two Zuls in conversation say that the Queen Mother would be arriving at the end of next week and she wants to witness the progress the city has made. They spoke of the need to protect her from enemy attack. Please, don't tell anyone else. We could get killed for telling you."

"I swear on my ancestors' graves that nothing will happen to you or your sisters." Alabi said, his voice low and resonant with conviction. He followed them back to their home, ensuring they arrived safely through the treacherous thoroughfares. Fara convinced Alabi to stay for the afternoon. She pulled him by his roughened, callous hands and dragged him inside.

"We would ask you to stay for dinner, but we're not

even sure if we will have dinner," Imade said with a dry chuckle as she offered Alabi somewhere to sit. The smell of human waste permeated the air, but Alabi thought it smelled better than the suffocating, oily stench of factory residue.

"How did you find this place?" Alabi asked, his eyes tracing the jagged cracks in the walls.

"Oh, it was hard," Leila said. Her voice felt small and fragile against the backdrop of the city's roar outside. "Nearly every spot we found was stolen from us. You know, since we are children—and we are also girls. We slept on the streets many times, but Imade always believed we could secure an abandoned warehouse or something of the sort. We almost had this spot taken too, because strays like us are desperately looking for a roof over their heads. We could share, but they never treat us right."

Alabi settled in the chair, the wood groaning under his weight. "How do you ward off thieves, then?"

"Imade got some charms from Zaza. They repel those who wish us bad. That is why we are so free with you, because it didn't ward you off. It means we can trust you."

"You said you came here to find your father," Imade said to Alabi. Her eyes searched his with an intensity that made him feel vulnerable. "What happened to him?"

Alabi hesitated, the memories of the raid flickering like a dying candle in his mind's eye.

"You can trust us," Imade said.

Inhaling deeply, Alabi said, "He was captured, nine years ago, when the automatons raided my village. I received word that he is here, working in the city, but it's been three weeks and there's no sign of him."

"And your best bet to find him is to find the resistance? Those people are murderers."

"It is my only option."

"My mother was captured too," Imade said, the words falling like heavy pavestones. "She was from the Benin Empire."

"The one with the impenetrable walls?"

Everyone in the region knew about the inaccessible walls of the Benin Empire and the shimmering, imperceptible field that prevented anyone from flying in. Its borders used to be open for people across the world to learn and explore their culture, but something happened that made them reclusive and unresponsive. Alabi's father was once interested in discovering the empire's secrets, as they were known for their divine craftsmanship and technological breakthroughs that bordered on the impossible.

"Yes, that one." Imade said. Her voice dipped into a reverent hush. "She used to be a trader, those days when Èkó was still a thriving port city. It was during one of her dealings that she met my father and fell in love with him. When the Benin Empire sent word to their children scattered abroad to return before the walls were sealed, my mother refused. She wouldn't leave us. Even then, she never renounced her culture. She would weave our history into songs, whispering them until they were etched into my soul."

Imade closed her eyes and hummed a melody that felt at once strange and familiar, an ancient and storied tune heavy with loss. She sang: *"My little Imade. Descendant of Ozuere. Daughter of Adesua. May the ancestors guide you wherever you go."*

"In under a year, the invasion happened and my father was murdered. My mother was taken too, sold as a slave like some cheap commodity." Imade sighed, then coughed, the sound rattling in her chest. "I wish I could get a travel permit like you so I could find my mother, but women aren't allowed in the factories, the farms, or the plantations. And only the 'productive' can apply for the right to move."

She looked over to the younger girls under her care. "I'm sure you wonder why Fara and Leila don't look alike. I found Leila almost dead in an alley—a ghost of a girl, abandoned by her white father when the Europeans fled the automatons. Fara too was left in a calabash to die. At least, I have memories of life before the iron came. Leila and Fara don't. This grey, grinding world is all they've ever known."

Tears lingered in Imade's eyes and Leila rushed to dab them with the edge of her threadbare dress. Alabi considered the girls with fresh awareness and a fervid, aching desire to protect them. Fara settled on the floor beside Alabi and rested her head on his thigh with a quiet, trusting sigh.

"My little Imade," Imade softly sang, her voice a fragile thread in the dark. *"Descendant of Ozuere. Daughter of Adesua. May the ancestors guide you wherever you go."*

Alabi spent the next few days sharing whatever food he scrounged with the girls, easing the burden of looting for survival and visiting dangerous places for treasures. He taught them how to identify scraps with high trade value and where best to discover gadgets and rare clockwork components that would make Zaza brim with greed. In return, the girls introduced Alabi to hidden pathways void of automaton patrols and rooftops where the Orah were more likely to haunt the shadows. They also described ways to distract the metal guards by throwing decoys—small, weighted objects—in the opposite direction, urging Alabi to practice this technique until he could move without being seen throughout the city.

After a long day of tricking and avoiding automatons, Alabi wondered, "What are the Zuls like?"

"They're rich," Imade said, her lip curling in distaste. "I reckon one Zul's wealth is enough to feed a quarter of the city workers. But they're not the sharing type. Although, some of them toss out bread from their gilded carriages just to watch strays nearly fight themselves to death for the crusts. They see us as less than animals. They see us as entertainment."

"What do you think their motives are?" Alabi asked.

"Surely, it cannot all be for technology and bondservants."

"They do it because they believe in the Queen Mother's quest for order." Leila said, and the room went deathly still as everyone glanced at her.

Alabi shifted in his seat, the uneven floorboards complaining beneath him. "Tell me what you know."

"There's this Zul called Ulman who used to wander the city in a heavy, charcoal-black carriage. He passed by workshops sometimes, watching the workers as they performed their duties with a strange, silent intensity. Fara has found him giving away tiny sacks of money in secret, or leaving flour and rice in shadowed corners of the streets for strays and workers to find."

"Hmmm. Do you think he feels some kind of pity for us?" Alabi asked, his skepticism warring with his hunger.

"Could be," Leila said. "He seemed like a kind man, but he was also loyal to the Queen Mother's cause. And for that reason, we couldn't completely trust him."

"Ulman tried to isolate Leila, to turn her away from us," Imade added. Her voice had hardened into a protective edge. "He found Leila while she was on the lookout and took interest in her—setting up meeting times and offering her food and new clothes like a man luring a bird into a cage." She shook herself free of the memories. "It is because of his generosity that strays never try to rob his carriage."

"Ulman believed the Queen Mother's quest would put an end to the chaos of inevitability," Leila said, her eyes distant, as if reciting a sermon she'd heard one too many times. "He believed the Queen Mother could establish order at the cost of humanity—that it is the only way."

"Violence should never be the only option," Imade said, her voice again cutting through the air like a blade. "The Kingdom of Benin runs a structured council system. There, every life is sacred. That kingdom is proof that you can have peace without the chains of slavery."

Leila nodded in agreement, as did Alabi and Fara. The mention of the council system felt like a prayer in the middle of a graveyard.

"How come I've never run into Ulman?" Alabi asked. He had been exploring the city for days and had never heard or seen him.

"We don't know," Fara replied, huddled closer to Alabi's side. "No one has seen him in months."

"He could've travelled somewhere," Leila said with a shrug.

"Or he could be dead," Imade said.

Alabi found a sheltered spot in the girls' home where they could plant vegetables and yams. He taught them how to dig into the stubborn earth, and how to water sparingly, and he devised a way to use human waste as manure to coax life from the rot. Fara immediately turned their tiny farm into a playground and began drawing pictures in the sand with the pointed end of a broken lever. She made stick drawings of parents and their four children. There was an additional character, fitted in between the two parents, with barely enough room for a torso. Alabi and the girls crouched low, trying to make out the caricatures.

"That's me, Fara, Imade, and Alabi," Leila said, pointing to the spindly figures.

Imade giggled. "Why does Alabi have two heads?"

"That's his stomach," Fara said, scrunching her nose in a frown. "And those will be our parents. When all of this ends, we shall all live together in Alabi's village."

Alabi feigned a pout. "Who is the last person?" he asked, still playfully not over the fact that he had two heads. She turned her head up at him, squinting as she smiled. Her eyes shone bright with an innocent certainty that Alabi wished he could borrow.

"That's your father, silly," Fara said with a chuckle.

***

Once, Alabi returned to the shack to find Ige's sack exposed and the room empty. Out of curiosity, he edged towards it, arms hovering like a bird of prey, testing whether it was safe to continue. He had barely begun searching when he heard the unmistakable rhythmic clicks coming from inside the sack. Alabi sifted through the grimy contents and, to his utmost surprise, there lay his travel permit nestled in the bottom. His fingers trembled as he held it in the dim, dusty light. He checked the timer on the clock and compared it with the number of days he had been in the city. They matched.

Incoming footsteps snapped Alabi out of his shock. He slipped his permit into his pocket and hurried outside, his pulse thundering in his ears. Ige met him by the threshold. "Do you need anything?" he asked, his eyes narrow and searching.

"No," Alabi said. "I was about to rest when I heard a strange noise from the steel mill." He smiled a nervous smile that didn't quite reach his eyes. "I have to go see what it is."

"Be careful, Alabi. You don't need to investigate everything," Ige said, his voice low and gravelly with a warning Alabi finally understood, though he pushed past anyway. Ige shook his head as he watched him hurry away.

Alabi spent the night with Imade, Leila, and Fara. Fara was particularly excited to have him over and pestered him for stories of his past. Alabi narrated the moments where his father would place him on his shoulders and they would go to the markets together—times where the only scent that filled the air was of charred roasted fish and *efo riro*, when the only cries that they heard were of a naughty child getting whooped for disobeying their mother.

The girls' mouths watered at the mention of the cuisine. Alabi spent the majority of the night explaining what each tasted like: the soup's vibrant, peppery sweetness; the chewy, gelatinous texture of *pomo*; and the juicy, elastic taste of *shaki*. He spoke of his mother's fragrant basket of spices and how his father would boast of her cooking. He mentioned the unending blue sea and the variety of seashells scattered across the beige sand, the times where he and his friends would force two crabs to fight each other. The girls listened with rapt attention, their faces illuminated by the faint flickers of a nearby lantern. They'd take turns interrupting him in his stories, inquisitively exploring any parts they found peculiar. Fara was the first to fall asleep, and soon, they were all resting, breathing deeply and conjuring dreams of a happier life that, as he drifted, Alabi feared might never return.

Alabi couldn't easily forget what Ige did to him. His shock had long given way to a slow-boiling, defiant anger, and he found himself pondering the exact manner in which he would enact his revenge. He had tried to think himself out of the rising hatred that burned in his chest by justifying Ige's actions, but his mind refused to be pacified. He stirred in his sleep as thoughts of punishing Ige played in his mind. It didn't need to be a major punishment—just something that would draw a pint of blood, leave a scar that would forever remind Ige of the consequence of his greed.

Sunlight poured in through cracks in the walls but the girls were still asleep. Alabi unwrapped Fara's arms from his calves and made his way to the shack, his footsteps steady with purpose.

Ige had turned the place upside down in search of the permit when Alabi walked in. Dust motes flitted throughout the air, kicked up by Ige's frantic scrambling.

"Are you looking for something?"

Ige at first didn't acknowledge Alabi's presence, or the manner in which he spoke, low and calm. He was steadfast in his search until, suddenly, his eyes shot up and his temples creased in displeasure.

"You took it!" he said, pointing an accusing finger at Alabi. "Give it back, Alabi. It cost me an arm and a leg."

"You're absolutely deranged if you think I'm giving you my own travel permit. How could you even keep it from me? What kind of man are you?"

Ige pulled Alabi by his collar, the veins on his neck bulging like corded rope. "Don't try to act all morally upright, Alabi. You know how it is in this city. You do what needs to be done to survive. Now give it back before I send you to an early grave."

Alabi shoved him off, the force of his movement nearly upending the small table. "Don't touch me!"

"You don't get to tell me what to do, Alabi. You're just a naïve boy, wasting away in the city in search of a dead man."

Time seemed to curdle as Alabi's fist connected with Ige's jaw, sending him reeling backwards with a sickening thud. Alabi caught him before he could fall, ramming him into the ground. He grabbed him by the neck, squeezing with a strength born of three weeks of suppressed terror. Ige gasped for air, his face turning a bruised purple as he squirmed in pain, struggling in vain to break free from Alabi's vice-like grasp.

Blood smeared across Ige's mouth and filled the corners of his eyes, but Alabi didn't relent. He regarded him with burning rage, strangling him in anticipation of a final, popping sharp crack of bone when… he stopped. Alabi released Ige, leaving him coughing and wheezing on the dirt floor. He stumbled back, dazed by the dark depth of his anger.

Alabi fled the scene, his palms slick and shaky with regret. He hadn't gone far when he felt the ground quake. From a distance, he sighted four imposing clockwork horses pulling a large cart, surrounded by armoured automatons whose metallic joints hissed with steam. Alabi couldn't return to the shack, so he made his way to the girls' home, only to find the door hanging open and the room hollow.

Screams of terror broke out and Alabi scrambled to the window to find automaton soldiers shoving strays into a cart like livestock. They banged on the old buildings with heavy iron fists, demanding whoever was inside come out. Alabi snuck out through the window, jumping over rooftops as he searched for the girls. His heart raced. Where could they have gone? He followed their usual route, through foul alleyways and cracks in abandoned factories. He searched the rooftops and under carts, hoping he would hear their voices or see them coming towards him from afar. Yet there was nothing but the rhythmic, oppressive marching of the machines.

Suddenly, a gunshot cracked through the air and the shrieks of a familiar voice echoed nearby. Alabi instantly recognised Leila's voice. He hurried through the streets towards the sound but came upon a troop of automaton soldiers. They drew nearer to him, servos whirring as they leveled their black-barreled guns.

Alabi fumbled for his travel permit and thrust it forward. The machines paused, their glowing red ocular sensors scanning the document; the lights flickered and turned a cold, clinical green. Without a word, they pivoted and marched down a side path. Alabi seized the opportunity to find the girls. He trailed the cart's heavy tracks in the grime until he spotted a body splayed unnaturally near a heap of trash.

Tears glazed his eyes as he recognised Imade's body, the

vibrant life he had known drained away, blood trickling from a jagged hole in her chest. The rusted steel rod was still in her hand—a final, futile act of defiance. Her colour was ash-grey, but her skin was still warm from the fresh attack that had stolen her life. Alabi fell to his knees, the world spinning into a blur of greys and reds. A pang of nausea made his stomach twist violently, and he retched, purging the contents of his belly.

He willed himself to get back up. He had to find the others. Maybe if he kept moving, there was still hope. He staggered upwards, tears pouring down his cheeks as he propelled himself forward, placing one leaden foot in front of another.

It wasn't long before he found Fara lying in the dirt, her face turned toward the indifferent sky. Alabi scrambled towards her, his breath hitching in a sob of relief when he saw the slight rise and fall of her chest. But when he lifted her, his heart sank. The light in her eyes had vanished, replaced by a hollow, thousand-yard stare. She showed no expression, no recognition, as Alabi gathered her small, trembling frame into his arms and fled into the shadows.

4

Alabi never found Leila's body. After searching for days, he finally acknowledged the horrifying truth: she had been one of those taken. Fara hadn't spoken a word since the incident and spent most of her days staring at the ceiling with glassy, vacant eyes, unable to eat, or drink, or cry. Many times, she lay so unmoving that Alabi had to press his trembling fingers to her neck until he felt the faint, thready pulse confirm she was not dead.

On one of his few walks, Alabi overheard a muted discussion between two workers, stating that the street cleansing had happened by order of the Queen Mother to instil fear and dominance after the resistance razed her chemical plant. The government had waited for the smoke to clear and the memory of the explosion to fade before launching the attack.

Alabi knew their plan worked. Ever since the ambush, he barely left his sanctuary in the decrepit building, and even when he did, he didn't spend more than an hour outside for fear of death. Whenever he left home, he discovered a new body, surrounded by a low hum of insects—the discarded remains of a parent, a sibling, or a friend. The air reeked of blood and soot, and it felt like a dark cloud had settled over the city.

Alabi wanted to return home. The world was too wicked to bear. He wrestled with the idea that his father was truly alive, and even if he was, he expected the worst: perhaps a missing eye, a lost limb, or a soul shattered by suffering and ground down by the gears of the city.

Was it all even worth it? Was endangering his mother worth the cost of this nightmare? What if he'd just stayed home? Joining the resistance just to find his father wasn't a feasible option anymore. He needed to fully commit and actively fight back to destroy the machines that had crushed his friends.

Alabi thought of Imade often, and often, painfully, tried to imagine the manner in which she died. He tried to envision the look on her face, her unyielding resolve, her teeth clenched as she brandished her rod even when she knew she could not win. She died a brave girl, and although Fara hadn't spoken to him yet, he knew that she died protecting her. Alabi wondered if he possessed that same spark—if he could abandon his own hopes and dreams so others could fulfil theirs. He thought of Leila, who he presumed was taken as a glorified bondservant because of her European features. He whispered a plea to the ancestors that she was alive somewhere, and hoped to one day see her again under a clearer sky.

The day before the Queen Mother's ominous arrival,

Alabi handed Fara a sack of food that he had gathered during the past few days. "If the worst happens to me tomorrow, I want you to keep on living, for Imade. Don't let her death be in vain," he said. "I promise to come back to see you if everything goes well."

Fara embraced him, holding him so tight that Alabi could feel her tiny heart hammering against his chest.

Alabi was meandering through the hidden pathways when he heard the bone-deep thrum of heavy footsteps from armoured automatons. He sucked in a breath, following the sound carefully, navigating the labyrinthine alleys until he reached a clearing where brass stallions hauled a white carriage bearing the crown insignia. Behind the carriage were twelve armoured automaton soldiers riding independently on the backs of armoured horses.

Alabi caught himself hesitating. The easiest thing the automatons could do was kill him. The memory of Atobatele and Imade surfaced in his head. And then there was the revered Queen Mother, who was the monarch behind the invasion—the one with a legion of automaton soldiers at her command. Folks whispered in dark corners, deliberating whether she was human or metal, god or spirit, because no one had ever seen her face-to-face.

Alabi scouted the area for any sign of additional automatons and, surprisingly, there were none besides the entourage nearby. Alabi kept his eyes peeled. He continued to follow the carriage carefully through an alley when he sighted a cloaked girl concealing herself in the shadows. Beneath the hood were amber eyes the searing colour of a forge fire. The girl, slight and lithe, suddenly produced a dagger. She slunk around the rust-streaked backs of factories and soon outran the carriage, waiting for them at a corner with predatory patience.

Alabi went after her in sheer curiosity. The girl didn't seem to notice his presence as she still had her fiery eyes glued to the carriage. She clutched her weapon and, as the carriage came closer, charged towards it.

Upon spotting the girl, the armoured automatons pointed their rifles at her, trying to lock in on a target that moved like liquid, flowing from side to side. Just as they pulled the trigger, a cloud of acrid purple smoke exploded and the girl was gone. Two automatons dismounted with a hydraulic hiss to search for her, while the other ten cocked their guns.

The girl reappeared, slashing her dagger and making a clean cut through the synthetic tendons of three armoured horses. The horses flinched, throwing their metal riders across the road in a tangle of alloyed limbs. The remaining automatons opened fire in the direction of the horses, but the girl had disappeared again in a purple haze.

In the midst of the chaos, an armoured automaton noticed Alabi and aimed at him. Alabi bolted away, veering in a desperate attempt to replicate the hooded girl's moves. The bullets missed him by a hair's breadth as he hurried through an alley. At the other end, he noticed a wall of automatons guarding the alley's exit and entrance. He stopped in his tracks, his eyes searching for an escape route when the hooded girl appeared behind him, the air now smelling of ozone and spent powder.

The events that followed happened at the speed of a lightning strike. A silver bullet grazed Alabi's ribs, sending a searing line of fire through his side just as a cloud of thick purple smoke engulfed them. Strong, wiry arms pulled him into a hole, causing him to land in a suffocating pool of feathers. The sun had disappeared, replaced by the low, flickering glow of dull flames and a powerful narcotic stench that rendered Alabi's eyes heavy with sleep. The girl undid her cloak and Alabi could see her now, although through a distorted, blurry lens. He opened his mouth to speak but was quickly consumed by a ravaging darkness.

Alabi jolted awake to find himself in a dimly lit room, roughly roped to a bed exactly his size. Ragged breaths burst out of his lips as he wrestled with the coarse ropes that scratched his skin. Alabi's memory was a haze, but he recalled the strident crackle of automaton guns, the automatons cutting him off, and the hooded girl. Had he been captured by the resistance? Were they going to kill him? If so, why hadn't they killed him yet? He heard the sound of quick, pattering footsteps as the amber-eyed girl came into the room. Alabi could see her clearly now. She looked about eighteen, with kinky hair braided into chunky cornrows and a face that looked almost too innocent to wield a deadly dagger.

"Who do you work for?" the girl asked in a sharp, uncompromising tone as she pulled out her dagger.

Alabi shifted under the ropes. Whatever she was wielding could cut through automaton armour with the ease of a hot knife through wax. "N—No one," he said.

She stepped forward, making the blade graze his neck, drawing a few stinging drops of blood. "The sooner you confess, the better it will be for the both of us. Unless you want to be tortured by my compatriots. Those men will chop off your fingers like it's just another Tuesday."

"I swear on the gods, I'm telling the truth," Alabi said, panting, as beads of sweat formed on his cupid's bow. "My name is Alabi, and I am a traveller. You can confirm it from my travel permit."

The girl retracted her weapon to consider the travel permit, flipping it over in her palm. She wiped off the bloodstain on the dagger with a casual flick of her wrist.

"Travel permits can be stolen," she said. "I will ask you one more time: what were you doing following me? Who is trying to find us?"

"I am," Alabi said, his entire body drenched with sweat. "The automatons captured my father nine years ago, and he was recently spotted in one of the factories of Apapa."

The girl squinted in curiosity. "Is your father a member of the Orah resistance?"

"No. He is an inventor who is rumoured to be working in one of those high-security factories."

"What is his name?"

"Korede. Do you know him?" Alabi asked, his eyes wide in anticipation.

"No," she said. "I don't. If what you say is true, why loiter around the Queen Mother's carriage? Surely, your father couldn't have been among the entourage. Surely, you're not so stupid as to provoke the Queen's ire."

"I want to find my father, but I also want to join the resistance. That is why I've been searching for them. A few days ago, a dear friend of mine was shot by an automaton. She was just thirteen and was the sole protector of two young girls." Tears filled his eyes. "The night before she passed, we reminisced about the days before the invasion and imagined a future free of this horrible dictatorship. It hurts me beyond words that she didn't get to see that future. I couldn't protect her then, but I can protect others like her. Please… I'm telling the truth."

The girl let out a sigh of sheer exhaustion. "Your story is moving, but I still cannot trust you—not when nearly everyone in the city will sell us off for a morsel of bread."

She cut off the ropes, leaving only the ones that bound his wrists intact. Alabi's heart drummed to his footsteps as she led him through a cramped tunnel-way where a few tiny flames were the only source of light.

The resistance base smelled of damp earth and trapped human musk. In the semi-darkness of the tunnel-way, Alabi spotted industrial metal tools tossed into a corner, a washing line, and raffia mats stacked against the moist, clayey walls. He heard the muffled drone of whirring engines, the harsh, grating sounds of members sharpening their blades, and a loud sneeze. Rats the size of dogs watched Alabi and the girl from a far corner, light reflecting like tiny embers glowing in their eyes.

The pungent, choking scent of gunpowder wafted into Alabi's nostrils, and he shuddered. As the echoes of their footsteps faded and he entered the main chamber, he stopped—as did his heart—when he saw six men, each pointing iron-barrelled guns at him. A violent quiver of fear dashed through Alabi's spine.

"Uncle Uche—" the girl called, brushing past Alabi with a defiant tilt of her chin.

"What did I just hear, Ruka?" A man—Uncle Uche—emerged from the gloom and came into the light. "You tracked the Queen Mother's carriage and you tried to single-handedly defeat armoured automatons? Do you even think with that head of yours? We planned to not respond to the rumours, and you go about risking your life? Why do you never listen to me?"

"It was for a good cause, Uncle. I could've prevailed if it weren't for the reinforcements."

"You could have prevailed? It was a bloody trap, Ruka! The only reason you're not dead is because the gods took pity on you. I've said it time and time again: you're not fit to be on missions. You're reckless. You're incompetent—"

"Enough, Uncle! I brought someone. I found him snooping around, but he claims he's not a spy and was looking to join the resistance."

Uche proceeded further into the light, the flickering orange glow making his wrinkles deepen as he considered Alabi. He was a middle-aged man with streaks of grey hair threading through his anchor beard, and eyes that looked as though they'd seen a thousand betrayals.

"Of course, he will deny it. No spy will agree that he is a spy." Turning to Alabi, he said, "Tell me, boy, how did you know where to find the Queen Mother?" His voice was a low rasp that carried the weight of a command.

"I—a friend of mine—she overheard a conversation between two Zuls."

"Who is this friend, and how can we find her?" Uche asked, his tone now flat and dangerously expectant.

"She died during the incident last week. She was a

stray."

"So a dead girl told you where to find the Queen Mother's carriage? How befitting."

Uche stroked his beard, the sound of his coarse hair against his palm loud in the lingering silence. "Tell me, boy, why do you want to join our little rebel group? Most people would rather capture us and sell us off to the Queen Mother than join us."

"The automaton government took my father from me when I was nine. He resides somewhere in this city, and I am trying to find him."

Uche's brows raised in astonishment. "I was expecting some noble speech about how you want to fight for peace and independence." The men in the room chuckled, a dry, mirthless sound that echoed off the damp walls. "Nine years is a long time, boy. Your father is probably dead."

"No, sir," Alabi said, his voice steady despite the guns still trained on his chest. "An old friend spotted him a couple years ago." Alabi took a step forward, his shadow stretching long across the clayey floor. "Please, sir. Joining the resistance is punishable by treason. I would not risk my life unless it is something that I truly believe in; I accept that risk. Help me find my father and I swear on my ancestors' graves I will be at your service."

"You've barely been here ten minutes and you're already negotiating. This boy has guts," one of the men remarked, lowering his rifle about an inch.

Uche regarded Alabi with a riveted look and smirked. He motioned to his men, who held Alabi roughly in place. "You *really* want to join us, don't you?" Uche asked. Alabi's scalp prickled in fear, but he willed himself to respond. "Yes, sir."

"If you want to join us, you'll have to prove your strength."

Uche motioned to the men, who bared their fists in readiness to attack. Alabi struggled to free himself, but the iron-clad grip of the rebels was too tight. The first punch landed squarely in Alabi's jaw, then the second, and the third. Alabi folded in pain as blood sprayed out of his mouth and onto the dirt. The next thing that came was a knee kick to Alabi's gut. A numbing pang distorted Alabi's senses, but he could still hear the muffled voices of men laughing and mocking his decision to join the resistance. He struggled to raise his head, but the earth tilted amid spinning shadows. The last thing he felt was the cold, heavy grip of Uche's pistol as he slammed it into his face and rendered him unconscious.

Alabi woke up the second time to a pounding headache, muscle contusions, and brindled bruises all over his body. He found himself in a prison of some sort, with Ruka at the other end of the rusted barricade.

"I remember seeing your friend's body when I was scouting," Ruka said, her voice echoing slightly in the damp cell. "A thirteen-year-old girl? Usually with two others? I'd seen those girls a couple of times, but I never bothered to befriend them or ask for their names. I only watched from a distance, watched as they pulled through this rotten city. The Orahs do not relate with those outside the group. Out of caution, we do not risk getting attached.

"I've put in a good word for you, Alabi, but my uncle and the rest of us will make our own findings to prove that you are who you say you are. If we find out you're actually a spy, we will erase you from existence. In the meantime, get comfortable. You're going to be here for a while."

Alabi didn't know how many days had gone by since he last saw the sky. In the gloom of the underground prison, he received little food and water, and even when he did, he couldn't make out the figure feeding him or the shadowy contents of the calabash. One time he ate quickly, only for him to feel the sickening slosh of warm blood in his mouth. He spat it out and retched, his sore ribs twinging as he emptied the contents of his stomach. A group of men roared with laughter, their footsteps fading into the damp silence of the corridor. Alabi didn't stop tasting blood after that day; it became a metallic phantom on his tongue.

Occasionally, they would forget to light the dim lamp by his cell, and he would sleep and wake up in pitch darkness, the cold, slick bodies of earthworms squirming around his body.

In all of this, Alabi held on to the hope of finding his father, of returning to his mother and Fara. He immersed himself in daydreams where he escaped into perfect worlds and positive futures. For days, he relived his happiest memories, engaging in dialogue with invisible people as the lines between reality and dreamscape blurred until the stone walls felt like paper.

One day, the gates of the prison squeaked open and Alabi opened his arms to his mother, only to have his illusion shattered as Ruka led Alabi through a tunnel-way lit with oil lamps. All the while she spoke to him, her voice sounded like the distant rush of running water in Alabi's ears. It took Ruka leading him to a place where the sun's rays seeped through a narrow ventilation shaft for him to fully return to his senses.

"My uncle has summoned you to the meeting room this evening," Ruka said, her voice snapping crisp and clear. "Don't worry, we will tend to your wounds and have you fed properly before then."

The meeting room was about fifteen square metres, its air thick with the smell of old parchment and gun oil. On one wall was a board pinned with images of daggers, reclaimed artefacts, and a massive wall surrounding a city. Alabi recognised the city to be the Benin Empire—home to Imade's people.

A table with a large map was stationed at the centre of the room. On it were splotches of ink, with red markings representing places the automatons had raided. Itu Agan was marked; Apapa, too. The unmarked parts were so few—a shrinking archipelago of freedom—that he had to narrow his eyes to see them. In between exploring the meeting room and waiting for Uche, Alabi experienced intense, crushing waves of exhaustion.

Finally, Uche and his men strode into the room, settling on stools, forming a circle around the leader at the centre. The men mumbled among themselves, occasionally throwing suspicious glances at Alabi to make sure he wasn't listening. Alabi stayed in a corner, legs trembling, barely able to stand upright, and waited patiently to be called upon.

Eventually, Uche motioned to him and, once he was close enough, asked him again, "Do you still want to join the resistance?"

Even with the burning soreness in his chest, Alabi looked him dead in the eyes, his gaze unyielding. "Yes."

"Everyone in this room knows what it feels like to be ripped away from their families," Uche said, pouring himself a cup of palm wine before passing the earthenware gourd to Alabi and the rest of his men.

"The only way for us to end this tyranny is to fight back, and that is why I formed this resistance." Uche motioned to a pot-bellied man who brought him a polished black box. "To defeat the automatons, we need to have weapons powerful enough to annihilate them."

Inside the box was a double-edged dagger whose blade was etched with the intricate image of a mask. It was the same unearthly weapon Ruka had wielded the morning they met.

"Do you know what this is?" Uche asked, nudging Alabi with his gourd. Alabi shook his head. He scanned through the men for Ruka, but she wasn't there. If anyone was supposed to be in the meeting, it was her.

Uche scoffed. He smoothed the edge of the dagger and angled it above his head, letting the low light catch the dark, iridescent sheen of the metal. "This blade was formed from Kuname metal, the strongest alloy in African history. Kuname can only be found within the Kingdom of Benin."

"Have you ever met the people of Benin?" Alabi asked, his voice barely a whisper.

Uche sucked in a breath. "Not yet, boy. We have made several attempts to contact them but have gotten no response. They do not wish to join our quest for independence."

"That's because the automatons haven't conquered

their kingdom yet," the pot-bellied man said, and the rest of the men mumbled in bitter agreement.

"That's true, but it has been nine years since they first landed in our country," Uche said. "Years have passed and the automatons still haven't been able to breach the wall. They're practically invincible."

"Nothing's invincible," someone else said, his voice pointed and frustrated. "It's only a matter of time before that wall crumbles." A babble of voices filled the air as the men argued, but with a sharp wave of Uche's arm came silence.

"Let's focus on why we called this meeting, shall we?"

Uche turned to Alabi. "Now, your test is quite simple. We have gotten word that there is a Benin craftsman in the city who could help us establish contact. We know this because some of the recent metalwork has similar markings to the Kuname blade. Find out who it is."

Alabi felt privileged to witness the pink and golden hues of dawn. All those nights in pitch blackness had him narrowing his eyes and sticking to the shadows, his body still carrying the memory of the dungeon's chill. He was grateful for the wind in his face and the unpleasant smell of the city, which was much better than the stagnant air of an underground prison. He made his way to the workers' quarters in search of Zaza and found him in his usual corner, wearing dark-tinted goggles and haggling with a man who wanted to purchase a plated mechanical gauntlet. By the time the man was gone, Zaza had a wide smile on his face.

"Look who's back," Zaza said, his voice like dry parchment. "I see you've found your travel permit."

Alabi ignored his remarks. "I need information," he said in a low mutter. "And I'm willing to pay for it."

"I'm listening," Zaza said, straightening himself as the atmosphere between them clarified.

"Have you bought or sold any Benin artefacts lately?"

Zaza glanced over his shoulder, making sure no one was listening. "Before I answer: how much are you willing to bargain for this information?"

Alabi dipped his hand in his pocket and brought out a bundle of cowries he had stolen from an abandoned Zul carriage, the polished shells clinking softly. Zaza's eyes widened from behind the goggles.

"Where did you get that?" he questioned.

"It doesn't matter. Do you have the information or not?"

Zaza swallowed. "I've only sold one, recently—a bronze leopard. The person gave me a pristine knife in exchange, the finest craftsmanship I've ever seen."

"Do you still have the knife?"

"Yes, but it will cost you."

"Even just to look at it?"

"Nothing in this city is free. You know that more than anyone else by now," Zaza replied, a greedy edge to his tone.

Alabi groaned and added more cowries to his bundle. Zaza searched his jumbo sack for the knife, moving with an urgency he hadn't seen before. The knife didn't have the mask insignia, but it was forged with the same dark, iridescent hue, extremely similar in style to the Kuname blade.

"Do you remember anything about the person you sold the leopard to?"

Zaza stroked his chin. "Calloused hands, an expert at haggling, and he seemed to be a lover of history. Oh, and a blacksmith."

"One more thing," Alabi said, his voice still low, now purposeful. "I would need a Forge pass."

Zaza had one handy and, with a shrug, sold it to Alabi.

Satisfied with his findings, Alabi was turning to leave when Zaza said, "Something about you has changed. A word of advice: be watchful. People can spot the difference too."

The men exchanged a knowing look—a silent acknowledgement of the tenebrous secrets Alabi now carried—and for the first time, Zaza bade Alabi goodbye.

Alabi hung around the workers' Forge until it was time for their shifts to begin. He walked amidst them, following the route to the Forge where he would begin temporary work. At the entrance, a wrinkled man stopped Alabi, requesting a means of identification. Alabi presented him with his pass, but the man's calculating gaze didn't leave his face. Alabi introduced himself as Jimoh, who was seeking temporary work while travelling. He squeezed a couple of cowries into the man's weathered palm, and the man beamed. Within a minute, Jimoh was allowed inside.

Instantly, Alabi felt the stifling, intense heat of the furnace. About forty men were gearing up to start their day, each of them with soot-covered clothes and beefy, calloused hands. A number of blacksmiths cleaned their hammers, anvils, and shovels, the rhythmic clang of metal on metal already filling the air against the constant roaring drone of the forges, while the rest of them carried down buckets of coal in preparation for the workday.

Alabi joined the men to carry the buckets of coal but was painfully reminded of the internal injuries in his chest and stomach region. He resorted to a near-empty bucket and spent most of the shift spying on the workers, trying to deduce who it was by their level of artistry. Not surprisingly, every worker in the forge demonstrated a sufficient level of mastery and Alabi—because he wasn't an expert in the craft—couldn't tell who it was among the sea of sweat and iron.

He approached the man who had demanded his pass, and asked him who he thought the most skilled worker was. "What do you need them for?" the gatekeeper asked, his eyes narrowing in suspicion.

"I would really love to learn from them," Alabi said.

In total, he selected ten men and watched carefully how they went about their work. Alabi's interest in the craftsmanship of the ten blacksmiths attracted cursory glances, but they were soon distracted by the relentless need to complete their daily quota.

In the middle of the day, two automatons walked into the Forge, their sensors scanning the room for any disruption in the usual pattern of the day. Alabi was shovelling a pile of coal into a blazing furnace when the automatons arrived. A sharp tinge of fear ran down his spine as one of them watched Alabi work, its red ocular light reflecting off the soot on his skin. A few minutes later, the automatons exited the workshop, and Alabi breathed a shaky sigh of relief.

Among the shortlisted blacksmiths, Alabi noticed one of them with a yellowed tusk necklace. He observed him and instantly noticed the fluid difference with which he shaped metal, the masterful ease of his technique, and how he rhythmically banged his hammer on the glowing metal bars. He waited until the shift was over and, when they were heading to the workers' quarters, he returned to Zaza with a description of the man.

Zaza snapped his fingers. "That's the one."

Alabi reported to Uche that evening. "His name is Zak," he said. "I haven't spoken to him yet, but I'm sure it is him." Alabi went further to give a thorough description of Zak, detailing the necklace and the specific arc of his strike.

Uche didn't seem impressed at all. He maintained a bare, impenetrable expression. "You can leave the rest to us," he said, dismissing Alabi with a curt nod. "We'll take it from here."

Alabi found tallies on the walls of the resistance base, diagrams illustrating the Queen Mother's defeat and the resistance victory. His thoughts immediately drifted to Fara's drawings on the sand—to Leila and Imade's plans for the future. His chest tightened as tears ran down his face. If only he had been there, he would've protected them—or died trying.

Soon, he heard footsteps approaching and wiped his face dry. It was Ruka.

"Are you okay?" she asked, and Alabi nodded. "Good. Come with me."

Ruka took Alabi to the loft of an abandoned warehouse. Besides the rusted, dust-covered machines and an automaton torso suspended at the centre, the place was mostly bare. Alabi gazed at the automaton in wonder. On its chest were vicious, shearing marks deep enough to expose the intricate hollow insides.

"This is where I train, where I sit in silence, where I can

fully be myself. This is also where I scout," Ruka said, leading Alabi to the rooftop. It was the same place that Alabi had spotted Ruka for the first time, over a month ago. It was only a couple of weeks, but it felt like a year to Alabi.

"You seem to have perfected the art of stealth," Alabi said. "With your cloak and that smoke thing that you do."

Ruka smiled, "It's called a smoke bomb, and yes, it is my specialty."

"I cannot forget the way you slashed at that clockwork horse. I've never seen anyone fight armoured automatons like that. You were amazing."

"Thank you, Alabi. You're the first to think of me as amazing, rather than just a liability."

"You also don't have to look after me," Alabi said, noticing how often she lingered around.

Ruka sighed, "I don't have a choice. Since my vouch, my uncle has made me responsible for you. You're still under probation, and so you cannot be alone. Even during your mission, every step you took, every move you made was recorded. We have spies everywhere, hidden in the shadows and the steam, people ready to disqualify you over the slightest mistake. We don't get many new recruits, and so we have to be thorough when filtering them out. You make one mistake and someone is prepared to blow your brains out."

"Thank you, Ruka," Alabi said.

With scrunched eyebrows, Ruka asked, "For what?"

"For believing that I am who I say I am, and for putting in a good word for me. I would've still been wasting away if it wasn't for you."

"I'm doing this out of guilt, Alabi, not out of the kindness of my heart. When the armoured automatons ambushed the strays, I could've done something, saved someone. Instead, I remained underground."

Her features softened, and she sighed. "The automaton government planned to use the chaos to draw us out, just like the ploy with the Queen Mother's carriage. My uncle made sure I couldn't escape. He said it wasn't time for us to show ourselves. Every attack has to be premeditated, every risk calculated. That is how we have survived for so long."

Alabi couldn't understand the need for cold self-preservation when people's lives were at stake. What was the point of power if they couldn't save the vulnerable and underprivileged?

"I don't agree with it either," Ruka said, as if reading his mind. "But my uncle thinks otherwise. He considers me careless and says there are some things I will never understand."

Just then, Alabi had a sobering brainwave. "There's someone I need to see."

He hurried down from the roof and bolted in the direction of the decrepit building. When he finally squeezed into the hole, there was no one there. Alabi's heart thundered. He rushed out, scouring the streets for little Fara. Ruka followed without question, her movements a silent, predatory blur behind him. She stalked him curiously until they came to a heap of trash. Fara was perched on the heap, sobbing as she hugged Alabi.

"You're alive," she said, cupping his face, running her hands over his rough stubble.

"I'm alive thanks to her," Alabi said, pointing to Ruka, who was hesitant to show herself in the open light. Fara turned to Ruka and hugged her by the waist. "Thank you for not killing him," she said, tightening her embrace on a stiff, bewildered Ruka, who stood like a statue amidst the ruins.

5

The resistance hideout was a labyrinth of tunnels, consisting of several cramped quarters and dozens of exits leading to abandoned huts, wells, and root cellars throughout the city. So far, Ruka had only revealed two of the exits to Alabi, one of them leading to the loft where she surveyed the city from. On his next visit, Alabi circled the inert automaton in disbelief, pondering how a once-feared mechanical soldier was now reduced to a lifeless dummy, its gears frozen in a permanent scream.

"You must teach me how to defeat one," Alabi said to Ruka, who smiled in response.

"I began with fighting people," Ruka said. "They are safer to practise with."

Alabi scoffed. "But you wouldn't kill a person now, would you?"

There was a pregnant, weighted silence.

"You seem to have a good heart, Alabi. But you must understand that the world can be desperately wicked. I don't know how things work where you come from, but here, everyone is trying to survive. You either kill or be killed."

Alabi had heard those words before, from a man whom he thought was a friend. Ige had tried to warn Alabi of people like himself, but he was too stoic to listen, too grounded in his village-boy beliefs.

Ruka clapped her hands, the sound resounding sharply against the metal rafters. "Come, let's get on with training then."

Alabi gave a nod of agreement. "Show me your stance," she said.

Alabi angled his shoulder hesitantly, his fists clenched, his legs shoulder-width apart. Ruka corrected his posture without asking. She placed her hand on his hip, and then his shoulder. Though Ruka was shorter, her warmth enveloped him, and his body betrayed him with a sudden shiver.

"Now, I am going to lean into my stance, and you're going to attack. Just follow your instincts, and pretend that I am the enemy."

Alabi nodded in obedience, his breath shaky as he had never fought a woman before. Ruka assumed a fighting position, her fiery eyes showing no hesitation. Alabi mustered courage but, unfortunately, threw a clumsy punch that failed to follow through. Ruka dodged his strike with a fluid grace, answering with a sharp whack to his forearm. Alabi's arm stung.

"Don't hesitate, Alabi. Remember, I am the enemy."

Alabi's next strike was fuelled by frustration. He swung with more force, aiming for Ruka's abdomen. Ruka expertly dodged the attack; only this time, she didn't strike him back.

"Keep at it," Ruka said. "Try to land a strike."

Alabi moved closer. He swung again, each punch stronger than the last. Ruka shifted just a hair's breadth before his fist could meet her jaw.

Alabi lunged, and Ruka pivoted. He feigned a low strike, drawing Ruka towards the ground. Ruka reacted quickly, crouching in a bid to catch his fist. When Alabi didn't follow through, she gasped. Alabi's leg was in the air, winding up for a powerful kick. At the last second, his resolve faltered.

Ruka caught his leg and swept it aside, sending him to the ground with a dull thud.

"Why did you stop?" she asked, more angry than relieved.

Alabi responded with a groan as he lifted himself up, the dust of the warehouse clinging to his sweat-slicked skin.

"We will try again," Ruka said, fierce eyes meeting Alabi's. "If you falter again, I will hurt you."

Alabi's training continued for the next few days. Since he'd found a caregiver for Fara, it was one of the few things that kept him busy besides wandering aimlessly in search of his father. Soon, he got better at anticipating Ruka's moves. She had become a familiar opponent, and he a better fighter.

The first time Alabi floored Ruka, he celebrated with a boyish victory dance. Ruka swept his legs in the middle of his dance and sent him crashing down. They remained on the floor, shoulders touching as they mocked each other. Alabi's gaze met Ruka's, lingering longer than intended until his travel permit ticked with a sharp, mechanical click, reminding him that he only had seven days left.

He jumped up, his heart sinking. "I have to go," he said as he left the training area. Ruka lingered for a moment, considering letting him leave unshadowed, before scooping up her pack and tailing after him.

Alabi kept asking Uche when he could visit the high-security factories, but Uche kept brushing it off. Zaza, despite his expertise, couldn't provide a pass for those factories either. Soon, it dawned on Alabi that the resistance didn't want him tagging along on the more dangerous missions. Ruka explained that it was part of his probation, but Alabi couldn't handle the suffocating suspense anymore. Every evening, he went to the meeting room, waiting to be called on, but he never was. Many times, they would force him out, sending him to do minor tasks like gathering information and intercepting automaton movement patterns.

Alabi perceived their meetings to be chaotic, with clashing beliefs and yelling, but a common hatred for the automaton government bound them together. There seemed to be a major cause of their arguments, and it was their idleness—the growing, bitter feeling that the resistance was not doing enough.

"You asked me if you could plant the bombs around the factory, and I said no," Uche said, during one of their chaotic meetings. "For the hundredth time, Kalu, we are not risking the lives of these factory workers!"

"We cannot stand idly either, Uche," Kalu said, his rumbling voice filling the room like distant thunder. "The more time we waste, the greater the cost."

"We are talking about hundreds of people," Uche said, his voice strained with the severity of an impossible choice.

"But we will save hundreds of thousands more."

The other men began to mumble, some of them frowning while others nodded in grim approval.

Uche raised his palm with force, silencing the crowd. "No!" he said, shaking his head vigorously. "We are the Orah resistance for a reason. We should not gamble with human lives. *We* are not like the Queen Mother."

Uche looked around at the faces that looked back at him, the low flicker of warm light reflecting on their pupils. His gaze drifted to Kalu.

"Do you understand me?" His question hung in the air, thick with a tension that threatened to snap.

Kalu managed a nod, stiffly.

Kalu's thought process made Alabi's skin crawl. The man reminded him of Ige—a man who would've liked to play god. The noise of the meeting faded as Alabi remembered that time was not on his side. He slipped out of the meeting room, and stopped by Ruka's room. She was his only hope of coming up with a solution. At Ruka's door, he heard muffled but heated voices.

"I cannot keep waiting on the sidelines when my nation needs me. I am a skilled fighter, and I am much more capable than you and most of the men in this resistance," Ruka said, her voice vibrating with a barely suppressed fury.

"So what are you going to do, Ruka?"

"I will create my own missions, Tokunbo. You can go tell my uncle if you want. You seem to be very loyal to him. While you're at it, why don't you wipe his arse too?"

"Please, don't think of me in that manner. All I did was for your safety. Your uncle would have had me thrown in a cell if you didn't return from your escapade with the Queen Mother's carriage."

"I trusted you, Tokunbo, and you betrayed me. I will never forgive you for that. Now, leave! I want to be alone."

Alabi hurried away, pivoting into the shadows just when the door swung open. As soon as he was sure Tokunbo was gone, Alabi knocked on Ruka's door.

"Go away, Tokunbo!" she said.

"It's Alabi."

"Oh."

Ruka let out an exasperated sigh before unlocking the door. The dim light of her room revealed eyes that were still bright with anger.

"I want to join you," Alabi said, his voice low and unwavering. "And I agree with everything you said. You deserve to be at those meetings and at the front lines of every mission."

Ruka shook her head. "It's too dangerous."

"For the two of us, it won't be. We can help each other. Please, Ruka…"

"You do realise that the resistance leader is my uncle and I can evade punishment. If you are caught in this mission, Alabi, I don't know what they'll do to you."

Alabi dodged the negative thoughts that invaded his mind. He wasn't going to get caught. He was sure of it. "I understand," he said, accepting the weight of the gamble. She stepped back slowly to let him in; this secret would bind them together as tightly as any iron shackle.

"Well, then, so be it."

"There are four types of automatons," Ruka began. "The most dangerous kind is the Azix. They are larger than the average soldier, and seem to have intelligence of their own. They can communicate in our local languages and make decisions within the limits of their programming. The Azix automatons were at the front lines of the great invasion and helped to either negotiate or execute most of our leaders. I'm sure you remember them, Alabi. I haven't encountered one in a while, but I believe that they have evolved over the years, becoming more predatory and precise."

Ruka took out a map and spread it on her table, smoothing all four corners of it.

"The automatons patrol the city in droves, but we have mastered their routine," Ruka said to Alabi as they looked at the map of Apapa. "Armoured automatons are just automaton soldiers covered in reinforced plating. They are stronger than the average soldier, but they can be easily tricked. They guard the centre and north wing of the city where the Zuls reside. These automatons can only stray a few metres from their stations. To make up for their limited movements, they have weapons that can inflict damage from a distance. They can detect the slightest sound and movement, and they are known for their unerring, mechanical shooting.

"The other type of automatons have no armour to speak of. These soldiers are the ones that move through the city. They are mindless and are the easiest class of automatons to defeat," Ruka continued. "But they can leave a station whenever they receive commands from their masters. The best way to bypass these automatons is to limit their visibility and to move with stealth. Memorise their patrol stations, estimate their numbers, use our underground networks, and move as soon as I give you the cue.

"The final category includes the clockwork horses, but they are new models, and so we aren't fully sure what their capabilities are.

"Today, we will be visiting one of those high-security factories you've been talking about. My uncle has been withholding valuable information from me, and I need to know what it is."

Ruka presented Alabi with a cloak, a factory pass, and a breastplate. "This breastplate is the only type of armour I could find," she said, shoving it at Alabi. "My uncle keeps the sophisticated technology stolen from our conquests hidden, and we only use them for high-risk missions. Put it under your blouse. It will keep you safe in case anything happens."

Alabi took off his shirt and donned the armour quickly, the cold metal feeling like a second, heavier skin.

"The cloak is to conceal your identity while we go to

the cart," Ruka said, avoiding Alabi's stare and glancing towards the wall. "The automatons might not be able to accurately differentiate between humans, but people can. Since we have become wanted, more people would wish to sell us out. Don't take it personally; they just want to survive. Just make sure you take off the cloak before you enter the factory."

Ruka undid her cloak, revealing the padded top she wore underneath. Because the factories didn't hire female workers, she needed to disguise her silhouette. She put on her beard and rubbed her palms in eagerness.

Ruka led Alabi through a damp tunnel-way filled with sweating metal pipes and valve wheels and finally came to an opening hidden with rotting planks where wafts of morning light seeped through. They arrived in an alley a few blocks away from the city center where Alabi's first real mission would take place. Ruka handed Alabi a few smoke bombs. "Take these too, but try your best not to inhale the fumes. We unfortunately don't have any spare respirators at the moment. Do not forget this entrance. It is in the alley by the steel mill." She pointed to a nearby steel mill for reference, its massive chimneys belching thick, soot-laden smoke into the dawn.

"Good luck," Alabi said as he put on the cloak.

"Good hunting," Ruka replied, her voice encouraging, but Alabi could see the concern in her eyes. Only his mother ever looked at him that way.

His heart raced as he struggled to recall everything Ruka had taught him. The position of the armoured automatons, the length of their strides, the size of their platoons, how to use the smoke bombs—he walked himself through each and every lethal detail Ruka had taught him.

Alabi and Ruka proceeded towards the factory by camouflaging in the shadows, pinning their backs against walls and waiting for patrol guards to march by. A stray cat caught Alabi's glance, but it was understanding enough to not draw attention to them. Ruka growled at it and it scampered away with a frightened howl.

Finally, Alabi could see the factory up close. It stood two hundred yards away: an enormous plant where billows of smoke escaped from within fortified brick walls and barbed-wire fences. At the centre of the plant was a metallic frame, shaped like a massive ball, that extended a little higher than the fences. Alabi couldn't make out exactly what it was. He spotted a huddle of heavily armed automaton soldiers at the entrance, their plates polished to a menacing coppery sheen.

They swiftly crept close to the steel gates of the factory. Two Azix automatons with red orbs for eyes guarded the door. The orbs pulsed with a low, rhythmic hum, scanning the horizon for heat signatures in the outline of intruders. Alabi and Ruka lingered out of sight until they spotted eight horse-drawn wagons moving towards the factory. One of the wagoners, a trusted resistance member, motioned to them. Ruka shot the man a couple of swift hand signals and, using the wagons and horses to hide themselves, they crept towards the man. Just as the automatons weren't looking, Alabi switched places with him while Ruka climbed into the passenger's seat.

The gates of the factory screeched open with the sound of grinding iron. The automatons performed a thorough search and scrutinised their passes. When they found nothing implicating, they allowed them passage. Alabi tightened his hands on the reins, palms sweaty. A set of human guards searched through Alabi's wagon. One of them had his eyes fixed suspiciously on Ruka as he fingered his gun. Ruka stayed still, a coiled spring ready to snap. Alabi did the same, maintaining composure and stifling the fear that eroded his mind. Once they were cleared, Alabi let out a quiet sigh of relief. Ruka and Alabi alighted and, like the other men, began offloading the supplies.

Alabi scrutinised the factory while he unpacked. There was a massive plant that resembled a monstrous rust-coloured engine, with several parts chugging and whistling, yet that wasn't what made Alabi quiver. At the edge of the compound, several workers mounted sky-high scaffolding and were modifying what looked like a giant automaton. Only the giant's head was incomplete; the rest of its body shone like glass under the midmorning sun. It stood at least forty feet tall, a colossus of brass and piston.

Alabi shuddered. How would someone—anyone—

fight against that? Ruka saw it too, her eyes widening in amazement that bordered on terror.

Alabi had almost finished unpacking when he saw multiple people staring at him and whispering among themselves. He wondered if they had noticed his inexperience from his shaky hands. Despite the stares, Alabi kept his cool, keeping his head low while surveying the factory from the corner of his eye. A quick glance at the workers, and he could tell that his father was not in the compound.

He needed to check inside. "We will leave soon," Alabi whispered to Ruka. "Just give me a little more time."

"You've got people looking at you, Alabi. We need to go. Now."

"I can't."

Alabi waited for a distraction to creep into the factory. There, rows of workers were soldering, screwing, and assembling automaton parts in a rhythmic, soul-crushing cadence. Alabi was scanning the place, when someone held his wrist in a vice-like grip.

"I know you're not supposed to be here," the person said. "Leave while you still can."

Alabi's breathing grew heavy as he tried to shake his arms free. The man oozed oil and sweat and had eyes like circular pools of tar. The heavy, hydraulic strides of an Azix automaton punctuated their conversation.

"These workers have experienced enough loss. They do not have the patience for intruders. The automatons are coming. Leave," the man said, leaving Alabi with his heart in his stomach.

Alabi sensed people staring at him; he could hear their whispers, could feel their hostility towards him, but most of all, Alabi felt the proximity of the machines. *Leave!* the man's voice echoed in his mind. Time seemed to slow down as Alabi whipped around and came face-to-face with the Axiz automaton.

"Identify yourself," it said, its voice a grating, synthesized baritone as it smoothed the brass pistol in its grasp. Blocking the entrance, the automaton towered over Alabi, waiting for a response. Alabi pretended to search for his pass. He knew his best chance was to remain calm, to cause a diversion so he could escape. He looked between the automaton, his empty hands, and the nearest exit.

He had calculated his moves and positioned himself to flee when a metal appendage crashed into the automaton's head, startling Alabi and the workers.

"Run!" Ruka screamed, and immediately, Alabi took flight, racing past the staggering machine and returning outside, where a platoon of soldiers was already preparing to attack. Alabi threw his smoke bombs, but the automatons searched on, red gazes piercing through the thick swirl of smoke, fog, and steam.

The automatons fired in spite of the fog, spraying silver bullets in the direction they expected Alabi and Ruka to be. Bullets clanged against metalwork, horses neighed in apprehension, workers screamed and ducked and fell to the ground. When the smoke thinned, Alabi was sprinting towards the underground opening by the steel mill, blood gushing from his nose and his lungs burning with every ragged breath.

There was first pitch blackness, then a flicker of candlelight. A jolting pain spread throughout Alabi's body as he stirred awake. He blinked until his vision was clear and he realised he was back in Ruka's room. Ruka sat beside him, her fingers white-knuckled as they clutched the cloak she had given to him.

"You're awake," she said, relief coating her voice. Alabi tried to get up, but his body felt like lead. "Rest," Ruka muttered. "You, Alabi, have got to be one of the bravest or dumbest men I've ever met."

Alabi scoffed. "How am I not dead?"

"The answer is obvious," Ruka said, gesturing to herself. "I intervened. The incident caused minor casualties; thankfully, none of the workers were terribly injured. I had to cover you as you returned to the hideout."

Alabi's mind went to the man who had warned him to run. He would never forget those dark eyes, that trembling voice, and the bruising tightness of his grip.

"My uncle wishes to see you at the meeting this evening."

Alabi's heart raced. "Does he know?"

"I don't know. He didn't say anything to me. You're not very good at covering your tracks, Alabi. And I thought I was the reckless one. What the hell were you thinking, going inside? I don't know how you managed it. You dodged the bullets, but the strain tore open old wounds, and you were bleeding internally again."

Tears filled Alabi's eyes as he stared at the ceiling, as he remembered the looks of spite the workers had thrown at him. They had reported him to the automatons and had betrayed their own people. And all for what? A day's worth of rations? Survival was a cruel master.

"I know it's not the right time, but I'm curious to know. Let's say you find your father. What comes next?" Ruka asked.

"I'm going to save him," he said. He wasn't sure how, but he was going to. When he was a child and he had problems—like when he tripped over a log and sprained his ankle or when he misplaced the cowries he took from his mother's wrapper—he would usually run to his father. His father had always been an intelligent and calculating man, a fabricator of solutions. Perhaps that was another reason why Alabi desperately wanted to see him: because a part of him felt they could find a way out of this nightmare together.

"What time is the daily meeting?" Alabi asked in

between pained puffs of breath.

"It happens in about two hours. Why?"

Alabi mustered all of his strength so he could sit up. "When it's time, please, take me to the meeting room."

Ruka nodded. She lined enough pillows behind Alabi's back so he could be more comfortable. Although Alabi felt weak and lightheaded, he couldn't help but stare at Ruka and wonder what her life was like. All she had done in the past few days was take care of him, and he wanted so badly to unravel her. His eyes traced the contours of her cheeks and the dark fullness of her lashes as she fed him morsels of *moi moi*.

"You still haven't told me what you were doing with the Kuname blade all those weeks ago. What was worth risking your life?" Alabi asked.

"You should be resting, Alabi, not asking questions like this."

"I don't know what your uncle's decision will be. Who knows, he might even kill me. This might be the only time we have this conversation."

Ruka sighed and played with her fingers. Her brows were drawn lower, pulled closer together. "I thought I could end everything with a single slash, but I was wrong. The automaton government has a bias against women. They rarely hire us to work in the factories, and they pretend we are invisible. They prefer that we 'breed' the next generation of workers and service the existing ones—most of us are captured and sold as maids to the Zuls. It feels ironic how someone or something can be called the Queen Mother, yet be so dismissive of women."

Alabi groaned as he straightened himself. "Everyone feels resentment for all the Queen Mother has put us through, but I don't think anyone has ever had the guts to attack her entourage. I've never seen anyone display such bravery, Ruka. You're a firebrand."

Her lips formed a small smile. "Thank you, Alabi. You are very kind."

There was a brief moment of silence.

"Tell me, Alabi," Ruka said. "If our homes had never been invaded. If you had the chance to become anything in life, what would you be?"

Alabi let the words sink into his head like an effervescent tablet. "I want to be a fisherman, like my father. I would've loved to also build machines like him, but I've tried. I just don't have it in me. I can only make simple tools and metal parts. That is how far I can go."

"You speak about your father so much, it's heartwarming."

Alabi feigned a chuckle. "What about you, Ruka? What would have been your dream?"

Ruka's eyes sparkled. "I would've loved to be an artist, but since the invasion started, all I have ever wanted to do was fight," she said.

The spark in her eyes disappeared and her lips formed a

thin, hard line as she stared at the ground. "I was nine years old when the automatons invaded my town. My parents were out for an event and I pretended to be sick so I could stay home and draw. While I was in the yard sketching on a slate, I saw giant, brass-bellied dirigibles floating in the sky. It was the most astonishing sight and I rushed to follow it. That was when I spotted the Queen Mother.

"She was about six feet tall but looked more human than her soldiers. Her eyes were a piercing, preternatural purple and she wore a tight-fitted gown of black leather. I remember her golden metal body and long black hair, almost reaching her waist. She seemed so captivating and yet so frightening. I was so afraid, I couldn't move. Then my mother appeared out of nowhere. She picked up a cutlass and charged towards the Queen Mother. Automaton soldiers came to the Queen's defense, but they didn't fire until she gave the order. So there my mother was, brandishing her weapon with gritted teeth, fighting the towering, steam-venting soldiers that towered over her. I knew, even as a little girl, that the cutlass wouldn't cut them. Still, I wasn't surprised by my mother's bravery. She had always been the fiercest person that I knew and was like wildfire to those who challenged her.

"I begged the Queen Mother not to hurt my mother. Yes, my mother was tough and brave, but I knew deep down she couldn't win that fight. The Queen Mother crouched to wipe my tears and turned me away from my mother and the automatons." Ruka's voice cracked. "I heard two shots, and that was it. My mother was gone. It felt like someone had turned off the lights, like the world had somehow paused and I was gliding in an abyss of rage and sadness. That was nine years ago, and I've had nightmares ever since that day."

Alabi reached for Ruka's hand and held it. He used his other hand to wipe the tears that dropped from her face. They locked eyes, and a wordless exchange ensued. Alabi was far too weak to pull her in for a hug, but he somehow knew that his feverish touch had provided her comfort, and he was happy with that.

Ruka supported Alabi's gait as he made his way to the gathering of men seated in a semicircle. Their eyes trailed him as he lowered himself into his chair. Alabi felt puny amidst them, like a naughty child about to be scolded by a group of elders. There were a few seconds of stillness when Alabi could hear the frantic thrum of his own pulse. Sweat flooded his body as the stale, soot-tainted underground air made him woozy.

"Sir, I..." Alabi said, but Uche stopped him with a sharp wave of his hand.

Looking at Alabi, he said calmly, "The giant you saw is

one of the automaton government's latest inventions. We can think of two reasons the Queen Mother would need a forty-foot tall automaton: superiority on the battlefield or assaulting fortifications. The Queen Mother has conquered every part of this nation except the mighty Benin Empire. It is still unclear how powerful the giant is, but if they succeed in invading Benin, we will have no hope of ending this tyranny. We have made several attempts to blow up the factory, but we risk killing hundreds of innocent people. The government knows that we show empathy towards our people and that destroying the factory is a move we are hesitant to make."

Uche turned to his left. "Tokunbo, have you finished repairing the Benin communicator?"

"It's not broken, sir," Tokunbo said, looking down at a brass device cluttered with copper coils. "It is just hard to establish a connection with the Benin Empire. It is like we don't have the right type of technology to contact them."

Uche clenched his teeth. "We will keep trying to contact the Benin people, but if we do not hear from them, then we will do what needs to be done. As for the incident..." Uche faced Alabi. "Ten workers had minor injuries from running to safety. One of the workers is here."

A man flashed his bandaged hand at Alabi, his forehead creasing as he maintained a tight, accusing grimace.

"The giant automaton you saw is overseen by an extremely skilled worker, a master technician who happened to be away at the Niger Delta when the incident happened. We've been trying to discover his identity for weeks, and we have finally been able to identify this master technician. His name is Korede, and he is one of the captives of an island village on the Eko coast."

Alabi felt a jolt of pure energy surge through his veins as he straightened himself.

"Yes, boy," Uche said "Your father is alive. It is for this reason that you are not spending the next few days in prison."

"Wh—what do you mean?" Alabi asked, his voice trembling with a mix of terror and hope.

Uche poured himself a cup from a gourd of palm wine. "When you first spoke of your father and his invention, I didn't understand the magnitude of your words. Now, I do. We will help you find him before the colossus is completed, but in return, you must do something for us. Don't worry, we are not going to hurt your father. We just want information. That's all."

"Consider it done," Alabi said.

"Oh, and next time you sneak into a facility without our knowledge, there will be drastic consequences," Uche said, and the injured factory worker cocked his gun, the click of the hammer foreboding. "Take this as a warning."

Alabi, when he was younger, spent most of his time watching his father build devices, but he was never allowed to touch them. Most of the materials were scarce and expensive to obtain, and Korede treated his inventions delicately, keeping them hidden and only allowing Alabi to gaze at them under his supervision. He, too, had validated his father's concern by mistakenly breaking three calabashes and one water pot, earning a thorough thrashing from his mother.

Korede had promised, however, that he would mentor Alabi when he got older—when his hands were less shaky and he was mature enough to handle things. That day never came, because Korede was whisked away, never to be seen again.

There was a hint of pride when Alabi heard that his father was behind the giant automaton, as he had always believed Korede would do great things. Yet, he couldn't help but feel a stinging disappointment that his father was working for the same government that had initiated their separation.

A horde of resistance members flooded the tunnel-way at dawn, their sweaty tang adding to the whiff of loam and fossorial dung that permeated the air. The Niger Delta was a few days away, but Alabi believed he could find a way to reach it before his permit expired.

"Alabi," Tokunbo called as he emerged from the shadows. He was broad and stout, with skin the colour of charcoal. His rough palms, stained with black oil, were an indication of his interest in mechanics. Tokunbo was one of those who seemed neutral, who didn't hate or bully him for wanting to join the resistance.

"I need you to come with me," Tokunbo said.

Alabi followed without question. He allowed himself to be led into another section of the underground fortress filled with brassworks, gears, and contraptions.

Tokunbo showed Alabi the communicator: a box-like device of copper and brass encasement, with an inbuilt conical speaker and a detachable earpiece.

"I do not remember where, but I think I've seen something similar before," said Alabi as his fingers grazed the machinery. "Could you tell me how it works?"

"Of course." Tokunbo replied. "The communicator uses this core to convert speech into signal waves, which travel through hidden towers to reach the Benin Empire's receivers. There, the message is broadcast through speakers. The same process applies when they respond to our message."

Tokunbo pointed out the pieces of the communicator and demonstrated turning it on. He pushed a button and the dial pointer jerked, swinging back and forth in a semicircle. Tokunbo turned the tuning dial and spoke into the machine.

"People of Benin, I am Tokunbo of the City of Factories, and I have a message for you." His voice crackled through the static, warbling and desperate.

Silence.

"They've never responded," Tokunbo said, his voice still captured in a flat echo against the communicator's resonant chamber. "Sometimes, I fear our messages have been intercepted, which is why I need your help, Alabi. I am one of the very few members of the resistance who has a formal education in science, and even with my years of study, my knowledge has been nowhere near that of the skilled workers of Apapa. People like your father are natural-born inventors, and although you haven't confirmed it yet, I believe you've inherited some of his skills."

Alabi let out a puff of air as he let Tokunbo's words simmer in his mind. The only invention Alabi could boast of was the binoculars, and even those took him several attempts to build. After his father left, Alabi had tried to recreate the steamboat, but he couldn't get the pressure valves to function. He had been more successful in his fishing and farming, and at creating simpler tools like ploughs, harpoons, and cultivators.

"I appreciate your faith in me, Tokunbo," Alabi said, "But I don't have the skills you require."

Tokunbo scoffed, "You haven't even tried anything. You said the communicator looks familiar. It must mean something."

Alabi shook his head. The communicator wasn't a toy he could experiment with. He couldn't take that risk with the resistance's only lifeline to outside the city.

"Well, if you ever change your mind, let me know. Getting through to the Kingdom of Benin could earn you the trust and respect of the resistance members, even Uche."

Alabi could not bear the weight of those words. It scared him that Tokunbo was counting on him, scared him that he might fail under the scrutiny of forty armed rebels.

"My father would've been the best person to help with this communicator," Alabi said. "But he is far away in the Niger Delta. I want to set off to find him, but I am conflicted. My travel permit doesn't allow me to leave the city of Apapa. I also fear that I might miss my father."

"You won't," Tokunbo said. "This isn't just your mission anymore, Alabi. We have spies scouting the skies too. You're not the only one interested in finding your father."

He took out a spare communicator, a smaller, palm-sized unit with a dull brass finish that Alabi could hide under his top. "Using this, we can receive whatever conversation you have with your father."

Alabi was tentative. Meeting his father should've been a tender, private moment, but his involvement with the resistance had stripped him of the privacy of such a vulnerable time. He took the communicator; the device felt heavy in his hand, a piece of the resistance's hope that he wasn't sure he could carry.

Tokunbo waved a cautionary finger. "Don't forget to put it on, Alabi."

At Ruka's surveying spot—his assigned post—Alabi watched watched the cloudless sky under sweltering heat, hoping to see an aircraft with his father in it, but there was nothing in the sky except a cloud of smoke and a flight of birds travelling west.

A tantalising scent wafted into Alabi's nostrils.

"You're going to go blind if you stare at the sun for too long," Ruka said, emerging behind him with a plate of roast plantain and a smattering of groundnuts. "How then will you find your father when you cannot see?"

Alabi smiled. "Don't worry. I've worked many hours under the sun; I can handle it. Where did you come from? How did I not hear you?"

"I'm the mistress of stealth, Alabi. You of all people should know that."

Alabi couldn't argue with her. Scouting for dirigibles was lonely, and he was grateful to have company.

"Take a break, eat," Ruka said. "You can't spend the entire day watching the sky."

Alabi smirked. "Thank you. You know, you remind me

of my mother, before the invasion. Especially those days when she would prepare tasty meals and serve them to my father in the backyard. Though, not before scolding him with a frown."

"What was he doing in the backyard?" Ruka asked, sitting beside him and leaning closer, the scent of char and a subtle, fruity fragrance hanging between them.

Alabi shrugged. "My father loved to invent, so he spent most of his free time in the backyard. He would draw objects on the mud walls before attempting to build them. I could never decipher those images—complex geometries of gears and pistons—but I admired the passion in his eyes when he settled down to create his machines."

Alabi took a bite of the roasted plantain, and a wave of hunger swelled through him. Within seconds, he had devoured everything on the plate. He thanked Ruka again—this time, noticing the piercing, analytical gaze she regarded him with. Alabi didn't want to fidget under her stare, so he shifted his gaze to the staggered roofs of the factories.

"How many more days do you have before your travel permit expires?" Ruka asked, her eyes falling on the ticking brass badge.

"Less than two days."

"So what happens then? What happens after you find your father?"

"I can talk to him, have him join the resistance."

"Hmm. And if he refuses?"

"My father risked his life to save his people when the invasion happened. I'm sure he will do it again."

"Yet your father is building a massive weapon that could burn down cities and potentially start a war."

Alabi's brows furrowed as he threw her a glance. "He doesn't have a choice, Ruka. None of us do."

"That is not true. The resistance can choose not to fight. We can choose to keep working our shifts and be allies of the government, but we refused. We chose this life, just as you chose to set off and find your father."

"What are you insinuating, Ruka? That my father is their ally?"

"I'm sorry to be the one to tell you this, but yes. Whoever you thought he was nine years ago isn't the person he is today."

"You know nothing about my father," Alabi said, his voice hardening.

"You're right. All I want is to free my people. You have less than two days before your permit expires, Alabi. And then, you will have to choose whether to return to your mother or fight with us," Ruka said, her gaze as steady as her blade. "Choose wisely."

Her fading footsteps announced her departure. Only then did Alabi let go of his mask of anger. He staggered backward, the weight of Ruka's words sinking in like lead anchors. He dropped onto a rusted metal protrusion on the roof, lost in thought. Ruka was right, his father did have a choice. The question was, what had forced his hand?

The night before Alabi's last day, with the moon obscured by a factory's eternal smog, he slipped on the communicator, considering it, the weight of it on his belt. The device felt cold against his skin. Its brass casing smelt of copper and old oil—the same scents as the metal men, the same technology as the oppressive regime. It was a bitter irony that the tools of his enemies would be their last bid for liberation.

6

Alabi looked through his borrowed binoculars, surveying the industrial city beneath him, sifting through plumes of steam ejecting through large chimneys. Through his lens, he spotted automatons patrolling the city, storming into workshops and demanding means of identification. Two strays, a boy and a girl, had been scampering across the street, evading automaton soldiers and stealing contraptions so they could trade them for food. Alabi watched them disappear into an alley, spectres in a city of gears.

Fourteen hours remained until the travel permit expired, and there was still no trace of a dirigible in the sky. Alabi paced around the roof as Ruka's words surfaced in his mind. She was like a single-edged blade: kind and nurturing in one way, and fierce in many other ways.

His heart raced as the timer on his badge ticked. He hadn't known anyone who didn't return after the time limit, as they feared the government far too much to even dare. Alabi thought of his mother back home. He imagined her at her usual spot, thinking of him.

"Bàámì," he said to himself, "Where are you?"

"Alabi..." Ruka called as she appeared behind him on the rooftop.

"You should go back, Ruka. Keep doing whatever it is you like to do and leave me alone," Alabi said. "I don't want to hear any more of your advice."

"Alabi, I—" Ruka called again, but he wouldn't look her way. He was depleted, soaked in sweat. The veins in his head throbbed, rhythmically pulsing like a pressurised pipe threatening to explode.

"Alabi!" Ruka insisted, this time tapping his shoulder. Alabi tightened his fists in frustration, ready to snap at her, when he heard, "Look up!"

Alabi's eyes shot up. Hidden behind a large cloud was a dirigible descending from the sky, its brass propellers churning the smoggy air. This was his last chance, Alabi thought as he hurried down from the building, ignoring Ruka's desperate pleas to wait for backup.

He hurried towards the factory—this time, with knowledge of the automaton patrol routes, underground networks, and alleyways. The factory gates were, as expected, guarded by armoured automatons, but Alabi was desperate. He threw a stone towards the automatons, and when they didn't budge, he threw metal parts instead. The automatons were heading his way when a cloud of purple smoke enveloped them. Alabi knew it was Ruka, but there was no time to acknowledge her.

He slipped into the factory and hid behind a scrap

hill. There, he watched as the passengers alighted from the blimp. Every organ in his body trembled in anticipation until, finally, a small, familiar man walked out. Tears streamed down Alabi's cheeks as he recognised the man to be his father, Korede. Korede went straight to the giant automaton to inspect it, unaware of the presence of his son.

It wasn't until Alabi raced towards him and called his name that Korede swivelled to see him. They stared at each other for several seconds, their eyes wide and unblinking. Then Alabi surged forward and pulled his father into a tight embrace. Alabi squeezed him, nails digging into his whitish-brown singlet. He felt the tenderness of his father's bones. The man who was always fishing and inventing, who had the chief and the rest of the villagers envying his strength and stature, now appeared smaller—withered by the shadow of the machines he was forced to build. Korede hugged Alabi back, tightening the embrace until they were fused together. Alabi struggled between laughing and crying as he pulled away to look at his father again.

"You've gotten so big!" Korede said, his face contorting as he sobbed. He cupped his son's face, "What about your mother? How's she?"

"She's alive. Heartbroken, but alive. We haven't been the same without you."

A metallic hand clamped on Alabi's wrist, jerking him back with hydraulic, mechanical force, spinning him away from his father to face an Azix automaton soldier. Alabi's eyes bulged in terror as crimson eyes stared down at him.

"Intruder," the automaton intoned in an emotionless voice. Sweat rushed down every pore in Alabi's body. This automaton carried the smell of copper and rotting flesh; on his fist was a smear of dried blood.

"Azix, stop!" Korede said, approaching the machine. "He's with me. He's my boy."

But the automaton wouldn't stop. It took out a brass pistol and aimed at Alabi's face, the barrel cold and final. Korede forced himself between the automaton and Alabi so that the gun touched his forehead.

"Stand down!" Korede said again, his voice louder as he stared into the eyes of Azix. The automaton's eyes blinked from red to black as it transferred its gaze to Korede. It lowered its gun.

"Identity confirmed: Korede," the Azix said and marched away, its joints hissing with steam. Alabi crumpled to the floor, pale with exhaustion. It took a few minutes to find his voice.

"Wh—what just happened?" Alabi asked, scanning his father's wrinkled face. His eyes fell on a golden badge pinned to his father's vest, its polished surface gleaming mockingly in the forge-light. Alabi's mouth went slack with confusion. "Bàámì, you have the travel permit?"

"Lower your voice, Alabi," Korede said. "We are in a factory. Don't lure Azix back here."

Alabi wiped his running nose with his knuckles.

"What's happening, Bàámì?" he asked in a whisper. "Why did that automaton listen to you? Why do you wear a golden permit?"

"I'll explain everything if you come with me," Korede said, leading his son outside the factory and to an area where dome-roofed apartments of cobblestone and polished copper loomed behind wrought-iron lattice gates. This was a world away from the soot-choked alleys Alabi had navigated. Gears shifted as Korede inserted a mechanical key, unlocking the gates and allowing them passage.

"What is this place?" Alabi asked, staring in awe.

"It's a private estate, a place where the Zul reside," his father said. "Come."

The air changed the moment Alabi and his father stepped into the estate. A cool breeze carried the scent of flower petals, fine wood, and grass. Every courtyard had a carpet of lush, freshly trimmed grasses and a section where homeowners parked their luxurious carriages and clockwork horses. The estate was serene; there was no sound of heavy machinery, chugging apparatuses, or billows of smoke rising from chimneys. The streets were tarred and the windows were squeaky clean, some of them revealing opulent leather furniture and the exquisite pets of a few of the residents.

Alabi had never seen anything like it. The front door of Korede's apartment swung open, and Alabi was left to gaze in wonder at the ample room, wide enough to fit in his entire hut. At the corners were single-hung windows through which light flowed, accentuating the crimson carpets, polished furniture, and king-sized bed that graced the apartment. Even the drapes were a heavy woven fabric, of a higher quality than Alabi's faded dashiki top.

Alabi looked out over the balcony balustrade and spotted a woman in a stiff corset smoking a pipe on her balcony while her slave stood like an unblinking fixture in the corner. She held the pipe with manicured hands, a cool breeze tousling her velvety hair as the sun gleamed on her milky bronze skin.

"Bàámì," Alabi said, transferring his gaze to his father. "Bàámì... you live here, with the Zul? You lived here while my mother and I mourned your absence?"

Korede regarded his son with a blank stare, as if taken aback by his words. "No, Alabi," he said, his voice trailing to catch up to his distant gaze as his eyes shifted over the privileged pavilion. "I've only lived here for a few months. I have been a factory worker for the past nine years. Only recently, after completing a big project, did I get a house and this golden permit."

Alabi grimaced at the badge, its shine now looking like the glint of a shackle. "The golden permit grants you access to a private house and what?"

"And freedom."

"Was it promised?" Alabi asked, his voice trailing off as he tried to stifle his bitter disappointment. "Did they promise you these benefits if you built them a giant?"

Korede's jaw dropped as his eyes shot over to his son's. "You know about that? How?"

Alabi's hands trembled in displeasure. "You created a weapon, Bàámì—a hulking monstrosity—for the ones who made us suffer, who took everything from us?" His voice rose in anger, echoing off the high, pristine ceilings.

"I'm doing this for you and your mother," his father protested, brows knitting in desperate defence. "The Queen Mother promised to liberate our entire family if I worked diligently. I am one of her most prized workers, one of the very few with this opportunity. One more year, and we could live like kings here. Please, son..."

"So we live like kings while the rest of our people die? While they suffer? But Bàámì, don't you think of this as betrayal?" Alabi asked as he felt his heart drop. It was hard to accept that this Korede was the same man who risked his life to save the village chief. What had happened to his father? Apapa had not just taken his father's labour; it had consumed his spirit.

"You're still young, Alabi," Korede said, a rising frustration in the glaze of his eyes. "You're still new to life. To thrive, you have to join the winning side, the stronger side.

We can never prevail against the Queen Mother. We never stood a chance to begin with. Her methods might be brutal, but they possess technology that surpasses ours. This is the only way."

Alabi paced around in thought, fingers grazing the smooth, unnatural surface of a study desk. The idea of aiding the automaton government made his insides curl. Those machines hadn't just scarred his body, but also his mind. They'd ripped from him his heritage, his life, his freedom. Alabi ruffled his hair and shook his head vigorously. He couldn't—wouldn't—let his father give in to the Queen Mother's lies.

"There's another way," Alabi said, grabbing his father's hands in appeal. "You already have the golden badge, and the automatons respond to you. You can use your knowledge of the government to destroy them. All you need are allies, people willing to join you in a revolution. Think about it, Bàámì: you should be trying to contact the Benin people, instead of working against them."

Korede broke free from his son's grasp. "The Benin people are selfish and naïve. They think they're better than everyone else. If they had shared their knowledge, we would've never had to go through this. I tried for years to contact them, but they never responded, not once. They do not care about us, so why should I care about them? If this vision of yours were so easy, we would've already been free. Tell me, son: where do I find the materials powerful enough to create weapons? How do I work on secret projects when automaton soldiers are lurking about?"

Alabi didn't want to speak of Uche's resistance, or the plans they'd set in motion. He wasn't sure whether Ruka and the others would be safe after his confession. And although the man who stood before him was his father, a shadow of doubt clouded Alabi's trust.

"Tell me, Bàámì, did you even think of me and my mother? Did you think of coming to see us, or sending us a message that you were okay?" Alabi asked as he looked around his father's apartment once more. The ostentatious luxury of the room felt like an insult.

"I tried to," Korede said.

"You tried to?! I spent three months searching for you! My mother suffered because of you!" Alabi yanked up his blouse. "Look at my scars! I had to work as a child under the harshest conditions. I cried myself to sleep every night, and you were here living a life of comfort?"

Korede laced his fingers together, his knuckles turning white. "Please, son, you have to understand. They took me away from my family, forced me to work in a factory for nine years. This is the only chance I got, the only glimmer of hope I could cling to. Don't you want us to live again as a family, together and free?"

Alabi's frown softened. It had always been his dream to live together like old times, but under the automaton government, there was no certainty that they would remain a family. They would always be third-class citizens, ruled by fear, forced to work for the rest of their lives as captives to their fatherland.

"At what cost is this dream of yours, Bàámì? We get to live on the blood of Atobatele and the village chief, both of whom loved you like their own. You were the village's pride. Now look at what you've become."

Tears formed in Korede's eyes, the weight of his son's words making his composure unsteady. He looked at his manicured hands as if they were stained with oil—or blood—he couldn't wash off.

"Life will never be good with the Queen Mother ruling us," Alabi said. "Deep down in your heart, you know that. Whether we live in a fancy cottage or a tiny hut, a slave will always remain a slave."

A sharp, rhythmic ticking sound in the ensuing silence drew Korede's eyes to Alabi's travel permit. He reached out to touch it but Alabi swayed away. "How much time do you have?" Korede asked.

"A few hours," Alabi said, wrestling with his thoughts, pondering the next step to take. He'd found his father. He'd done what he could, and yet he felt more alone than ever.

"Go. Run back home as fast as you can!" Korede said.

Alabi didn't move. He had only just arrived and still had much to say.

Korede held his son's face and looked deep into his eyes. "Do as I say, son. Hurry. Go be with your mother."

Alabi hesitated. Those were the exact words his father said to him nine years ago. After that, they didn't see each other again. He didn't even try to find them. Unlike Alabi, who travelled great lengths, his father never tried. How would he tell his mother that her husband had grown selfish—that he was alive and living comfortably while they endured daily torment?

The relentless ticking sounds of the travel permit cut him out of his thoughts. There was no time to wallow in his mistakes. What was most important was the way forward. He would get stronger, work harder to rebel against the forced servitude that had turned his father into someone he could not recognise. Alabi took one last look at Korede—the golden badge on his father's chest gleaming like a cold, metallic heart—and hurried out the door.

Alabi's boat made it to the brink of the village an hour and thirty minutes before his time expired. By then, the sun's intensity had decreased and a cool breeze drifted through the village. Alabi raced to his hut, the implacable gaze of automaton soldiers trailing him as he hurried past them.

When Alabi reached the hut, he called for his mother, but there was no response. He went to her room and found Labake sleeping. It was unlike her to be asleep in the afternoon unless she had bouts of malaria, but even then, the faintest noise was enough to wake her.

Eager to share his discovery, Alabi tapped his mother's shoulder until she opened her jaundiced, yellowed eyes. A wide smile spread across her face as she noticed her son, and she opened her bony arms to hug him.

"He's alive," Alabi whispered as he rested in her warm embrace. "I met my father. He is alive."

His mother's chest rose and fell like ocean waves, every lungful of air releasing a laboured, whistling hiss. Alabi took a step back so he could examine his mother. "Màámì, are you alright? Did you hear what I said?"

His mother gave a light nod and smiled again, the corners of her hollow eyes crinkling like dry parchment.

"Alabi… have you been eating?" she asked in a hoarse voice.

"Yes, Màámì," Alabi said with a sad smile. It pained him to return to find her in this infirm state. He smoothed her hair, tucking a braid behind her ear. "I'll be back. Let me go and get the village herbalist," Alabi said, preparing to leave.

"No, don't go," Labake said, as she slipped her hand in his. Her grip was frail, a whisper of the strength she once held. "Stay with me."

Alabi rubbed his mother's hand. "Don't worry, Màámì," he said. "You'll get better and you'll see your husband again. We'll be together again, I promise."

Labake said nothing, a hopeful smile never leaving her face. Her eyes held Alabi's with a lingering light until he finally crossed the threshold and stepped into the fading day.

He bolted out the door in search of the village herbalist, and was lucky to find him at the plantation farm, right when his shift was over. The herbalist regarded the news with urgency, leaping to his feet and rushing to Alabi's hut.

Alabi knew that his mother was gone when her eyes were once again clamped shut, her body unmoving. He approached and called his mother's name, his voice rising until it became a quavering howl, the gut-shattering bellow of a frightened animal. Tears clouded his vision as he placed his head on her chest and heard nothing but a hollow, internal silence.

The herbalist edged towards her, hesitant to touch. It was as if he could sense the absolute stillness in the air. He locked eyes briefly with Alabi, whose face was bloated and wet with tears, then he placed a finger beneath her nose and listened for a heartbeat.

"I'm so sorry, Alabi," he said, his voice a saddened, reverent whisper. "She's gone."

Alabi felt like the world had collapsed, like the earth had

been stripped of its colour. He fell to his knees and wept, letting out a cry so raw that it moved the herbalist to tears. For most of Alabi's life, he had feared losing his father, but he had never imagined his mother dying. Despite her sickness, he had always believed she would survive, just like she had always done. If only he had spent the last few days with her—if he wasn't so obsessed with finding his father—she might still be alive. The guilt felt like the crushing weight of his father's mechanical colossus, forcing all the air from his lungs as if he were being flattened by a hydraulic press.

Unable to stand, Alabi crawled to his mother and placed his head on her chest. Nothing mattered to him anymore. The world could crumble, and he wouldn't lift a finger to stop it. All of his resolve and ambitions had died with his mother. Maybe that was the Queen Mother's goal—to take and take until there was nothing left but a shell.

Alabi closed his eyes, not minding that flies perched on his skin or that ants were marching on his chest. He languished in his mother's fading warmth until he no longer heard the relentless, mocking clicks of the travel permit.

The next few days were a blur to Alabi, a continuum of wailing and working. His senses were distorted by waves of grief and regret, and by the excruciating reality of his mother's absence. Some of Alabi's coworkers whispered words of consolation to him, but Alabi couldn't bring himself to respond. His heart had been shattered into a million pieces. There was nothing left but the unbearable ache of her absence.

Alabi would normally not dwell on specific details of his past, but his mother's death had cut him so deep that the only way to begin healing was to plunge himself into an abyss of fond memories—memories of when his mother existed, of when she was in her happiest, most satisfied state.

Alabi remembered peering into the kitchen in anticipation, unable to resist the aroma of *efo riro* soup coming from the kitchen. His mother stood near the boiling cauldron, her face immersed in a cloud of steam as she opened the lid and stirred what was inside. Her hair beads clicked in a soft, rhythmic percussion as she nodded in satisfaction, pleased with what she saw in her pot. She tasted the food, raised a brow calculatingly, before adding salt and tasting again.

Alabi watched his mother in fascination, wondering how she could open the lid without a napkin. How was his mother's skin so resistant to heat? She whisked a fly away, reached for a calabash, and turned to Alabi.

"Go, call your father. Tell him the food is ready," she said.

Alabi hurried to the backyard and found his father gazing at the drawings on the mud wall, his temples creased in seriousness. Alabi edged closer to see.

"What's that, Bàámì?" he asked.

"It is a communicator," Korede replied.

"A komini… komenie…"

Korede scoffed. "Communicator," he corrected.

Alabi stared at the drawing, which resembled a cuboidal object with trailing cords attached to it.

"A kominigator," Alabi mumbled, as if saying the words would make them more understandable. He wanted to question the drawing further—to ask what its purpose had and why his father was glued to it—but his mother's voice pierced through his thoughts, reminding him that he was yet to deliver her message.

Alabi was about to speak about the food when he saw his mother glaring at him with her arms folded. "Your food is ready, Korede," she said to her husband.

"I'll be there in a minute," Korede said, unaware of his wife's lingering presence. She waited exactly a minute before speaking again—this time with a deeper frown and refolded arms. Alabi sensed the tension, but he wouldn't dare leave. Not when his mother was a walking ball of fury.

"Korede, if your food gets cold, I swear, I will never

make you a meal in my life again," she said. "I hope your machines can prepare soup." His mother stomped away, returning almost immediately to pull Alabi away by his ear.

Grown Alabi touched his ear. He would give anything to once again be chastised by his mother, to feel her touch, to hear her voice. He missed his father too. Regardless of how selfish he had become, he still wanted him close.

"Communicator," he breathed. The sun had just set after a long day of work; Alabi lit an oil lamp and carried it to the backyard. A gust of breeze tried to extinguish the fire, but Alabi shielded the lamp, treading slowly.

The back of the hut was filled with slates—sketches of machines his father had planned on making. A meddling lizard scurried away when Alabi came along. Underneath the stack of slates was a home for insects and a feeding ground for reptiles.

Alabi brushed his hands against the wall, but he found no sketch. Perhaps it had been washed off by the rain or buried under dust and dirt. He tried to wipe it with his fingers and immediately felt a hollow depression at the centre of the wall.

Alabi scanned his surroundings, but there was nothing but darkness and bush rats scavenging for food. He dropped the lamp and shoved a stick into the centre of the wall. A light shove was enough for him to create a hole. He dipped his hand into the opening and found a smattering of gears and brass equipment. Alabi was a curious and sloppy child, so it was understandable that his father would hide his inventions.

He brought out the gadgets one by one, inspecting each of them to ascertain their value. He noticed a machine glistening: a cylindrical object, wound by brass coils—a signal core. He observed the signal core, stunned by its craftsmanship, when he saw an emblem that reminded him of Ruka's dagger. At that moment, he had a flash of inspiration. He was going to build a communicator.

Alabi spent the next few days combing the village for materials, improvising, testing, and discarding as he went. Before long, he had fashioned a speaker from stretched animal skin and an earpiece from a local flute.

That same night, Alabi locked himself in his hut, and began to assemble, relying solely on his instincts and his understanding of how the individual parts functioned. He joined the objects together using glue, wax, and metal wires. After about three hours, he was left with a portable communicator.

Alabi switched it on. He jumped in triumph when it vibrated and shuddered to life. A piercing screech threw Alabi into a frenzy, and he rushed to drown the noise under a heap of clothes. Barely a minute later, he heard a muffled voice coming from the communicator. Alabi made sure to shut the windows and doors before taking his clothes off the device. The muffled voice spoke in an unfamiliar language—rhythmic and tonal—and seemed to be asking a question.

Alabi, afraid that he might miss his opportunity, blurted out, "Good evening… I am Alabi of Itu Agan and I wish to speak with the Benin people. I want to warn them of an impending assault."

A short silence ensued. Alabi was abruptly made aware of a rattling noise emanating from a shelf in his room. Alabi's heart raced. He needed to think fast—to say something, anything that would hold their attention. *"Little Imade,"* he said, his voice trembling as he recalled Imade's song in her native tongue. *"Descendant of Ozuere… Daughter of Adesua…"*

"Where did you hear those names?" the voice asked in his familiar language. Alabi breathed a sigh of relief when the responder switched to a dialect he could finally navigate.

"My friend taught me before she passed. Her mother was from your kingdom and was among those who remained in the city after you closed down your walls. Please, for the sake of Imade, for the sake of Adesua, hear me out. A giant automaton is under construction, and the Queen Mother plans to use it to invade your empire."

"Giants have never been able to breach our defenses. What makes this one different?"

"I suspect this weapon has been engineered specifically to counter your fortifications. If it doesn't break your walls, it will be the hammer that shatters your gates."

"How do you know all this?"

Alabi paused to wipe the droplets of sweat forming on his forehead. "I know because my father oversees the project and because I have been spying on them. For a few weeks, I was part of a resistance that tried in vain to contact you. We believe you can help us stop this slavery."

"Benin doesn't align itself with the rest of the world. We are our own people," the voice said, cold and isolationist.

"I understand. But if you do not join forces with us, then we will all be damned. They're building colossi now. No one is safe."

Another piercing screech—a violent surge of static—forced Alabi to clamp his ears shut. When the noise squelched and ceased, Alabi could no longer hear the voice. He toggled the switches and adjusted the brass coils many times, waiting until the first grey light of sunrise filtered through the cracks in his hut, but heard nothing. The signal core went cold.

The sky after a heavy rainfall was an ember-and-honey hue, the clouds stained with an occulted sunset. The cool wind lingered through the trees, taking leaves and dirt along with it. Alabi had just concluded his shift and was dripping wet when he spotted fresh footprints leading to his house. He rushed inside, wanting so badly for it to be his mother—a desperate, impossible hope—but the house was empty. It had been a hollow shell since she passed away.

Alabi dropped to his sleeping mat, his heart heavy with sorrow. Only when his head reached the floor did he realise that the air in the room felt different. The shelf where he had placed his makeshift invention was bare. The communicator was gone.

7

JULY 10, 1866
ITU AGAN VILLAGE, SNAKE ISLAND

Rays of sunlight crested the waves of the rippling blue sea where Alabi and a group of fishermen were casting their nets. Their task for that morning was to harvest as much fish as possible and store them in the village's food shelter. Alabi, fatigued from days of not eating, struggled to maintain hold of the net. One of his coworkers squeezed his shoulder. "Rest, I'll take care of it," the man said.

Suddenly, something blocked the sun, momentarily casting a shadow over Alabi's boat. Alabi felt a tinge of fear. He looked up and saw nothing but the vast blue sky and clouds wafting in the gentle breeze. Perhaps it was a trick of the light, he thought, but as he picked up his paddle and headed for the shore, the water quaked. Alabi paused, his heart thumping as he watched the unnatural surge of the current.

Beckoning to the other men, Alabi said, "There's something swimming towards the island." Within a minute, every fisherman's eye was on the undulating waves. Some of them squinted, trying to make out what was moving beneath the surging current. The water began to churn with mechanical precision, and five figures emerged from the sea. Each of them wore reinforced leather armour and copper masks that left only the backs of their heads vulnerable to attack. In their hands were spears, daggers, and embossed shields, and their feet were clad with solid, water-sealed boots.

Alabi's boat was the farthest from the shore, and so he was the most terrified of the bunch. One of the armoured strangers waded towards him, the water shedding off his copper visage like liquid silk. Angling his head, he put a finger to his masked lips, warning Alabi to stay quiet. From the structure of their bodies, Alabi could tell they were human, with varying hues of black and brown skin. But who were they, and what was their purpose on the island? He spotted something familiar engraved on their daggers and shields—the meticulous, ancient engraving of a mask, the revered emblem of the Benin people. A wave of electric excitement rushed through his body, instantly cauterizing the fear that had once tightened his chest.

The masked men signalled to one another with efficient, silent gestures and headed for the village, leaving Alabi and the fishermen behind them in the surf. Once they reached the shore, Alabi dashed toward the village to find that the troop of masked warriors had multiplied. Reinforcements descended from a rope that appeared to emerge from a shimmering rift in the sky—an anchor point for an invisible aircraft. Looking up, Alabi realised he was witnessing a Cloud Maker in action, a stealth vessel of myth and mist he had only ever known from his father's fables.

The entire village plunged into a cacophony of clashing iron as the Benin warriors fell upon every automaton in sight. The machines opened fire, but their silver bullets clattered harmlessly off the electromagnetic shields of the attackers.

One Benin warrior was a centralising whirlwind of precision. They lunged at the soldiers of the Queen Mother, slashing and jabbing with the fluid lethality of a clouded leopard. Black hydraulic fluid sprayed from the fractured joints of the machines until they were reduced to a sparking heap of useless metalwork.

The warrior removed their mask, and Alabi was surprised to see a woman whose face was marked by a vicious scar running across her left eye.

"Hey, you. Are you Alabi of Itu Agan?" the warrior asked, her gaze as cold as the spear in her hand. Alabi bowed low, his heart in his throat.

"Yes. I am the one you seek," he said.

The woman studied him for a heartbeat before spinning on her heel, her spear whistling as it cleaved through the brass chest-plate of an oncoming automaton.

"It's a pleasure to meet you, Alabi. I'm General Isoken. Stay close to me," she said. "I have to get you to the airship as quickly as possible." She tossed Alabi a heavy, bronze-tipped spear and a reinforced shield. "Use them well, Alabi, or die holding them," she commanded, her voice cutting through the din. "Channel all your pain and anger, and take back what these slavers have stolen from you!"

Troops of automaton soldiers dashed out from the village square, opening fire to kill every living thing in their path. The Benin warriors blocked the silver bullets with their vibrating shields, but innocent villagers were not so lucky. Cries of anguish broke from different corners of the village as dozens of men, women, and children dropped dead. The Benin warriors doubled their efforts, their blades singing and spears sibilant as they destroyed as many automatons as they could find.

Alabi, ignited by the senseless slaughter of his people, squeezed his spear, raised his shield, and lunged at an automaton. His stance felt strong, and he sprung forth like Ruka had taught him; the spear felt balanced, lithe, and natural to grip and extend. He hurled his entire weight behind the strike, thrusting the weapon into its chest and driving it so deep that viscous black goo immediately spewed forth from the opening.

The automaton's optical screen flickered erratically. With its last reserve of waning power, it attempted to grapple its way to freedom, but Alabi was unyielding. Planting his lead foot, he shoved the automaton into the wall of a mud house, driving it into the structure like a nail. Then, with clenched teeth and all his strength, Alabi dragged the spear violently downwards. Tiny sparks hissed as the blade sliced through the automaton's iron frame, tearing it open like a fish's belly. Alabi felt a rush of ecstasy when the automaton no longer moved, when it fell to the ground and its eyes flickered out and went dim. That kill was for his mother and the innocent people who had died in battle—for all the nights he had wailed and suffered and wished he had never been born.

In his moments of distraction, other automaton soldiers closed in, their eyes glowing luminous with murderous, crimson light. Alabi held his breath and tightened his grip, readying himself in a crouch. He was about to spring forth again when a platoon of Benin warriors emerged from behind him, overwhelming the automatons with precise stabs to their chests. Alabi didn't want to be left out. One kill wasn't enough. He picked up the spear once more, but as he proceeded towards the fray, General Isoken snagged the back of his blouse.

"That's enough," Isoken commanded, her voice firm against the roar of battle. "You have to head to the airship now, before it's too late."

Alabi nodded and followed the general to the centre of the village where the shimmering silhouette of the airship stood. Taking a final look at his village, Alabi wondered what would become of his people. Thanks to the Benin warriors, they might have won a battle, but a devastating war was brewing. He was separated from his father and had lost his mother; all that remained of his world was his village, a scarred patch of earth now choking on the black smoke and bitter grease of war.

"Don't worry about them," the woman said, her expression softening just enough to reveal a sliver of empathy. "We will make sure no one else is lost."

She signalled to her men before leading Alabi into the brass-lined belly of the airship. As the aircraft lifted into the sky, vibrating with the power of harnessed lightning, the general turned to Alabi. She leaned against a navigational console, her scarred eye fixed on him with intense focus.

"Now, Alabi of Itu Agan, where can we find this resistance you spoke of?"

Alabi pinned his back against a wall in an alley in Apapa and waited for a huddle of automaton soldiers to march past, their metal feet clanking rhythmically against the cobblestones. The aircraft was hidden behind the clouds, circling the area where the resistance hideout was. Alabi entered the opening by the forge, the air thick with the familiar scent of coal and hot iron, but as soon as he reached the hideout, he saw Ruka pointing a gun at him. Her amber eyes widened when she recognised Alabi.

"Why—what—h—how are you here?"

"There's no time to explain," Alabi said, his voice urgent. "Where's Uche?"

"He's at work. What do you need him for?"

Just then, they heard someone step into the shadows. Ruka raised her gun at the intruder, who also raised her weapon, placing the bronze end of her spear a hair's breadth away from Ruka's neck. When Ruka met the woman's eyes and saw the meticulous markings on her weapon, she lowered her pistol and stared in disbelief.

"This is General Isoken," Alabi said. "I found a way to contact the Benin people, but they need your uncle."

The General's gaze didn't leave Ruka. "Alert him," she said, retracting her spear with a sharp, metallic click. "There's no time to waste."

"I don't think they'll let him off his shift at this hour," Ruka said, her voice steady under General Isoken's inscrutable stare.

"Where is his workplace?" the general asked, her jaw set in a hard line.

"A few blocks away."

Isoken's frown deepened. "Show me."

Ruka, Alabi, and Isoken crouched in a corner, a few paces away from the workshop where Uche worked. The muffled sound of clanking metals drowned the heavy strides of automaton soldiers patrolling the area. Once they were out of sight, Isoken tightened the straps on her copper bracers and cracked her neck.

"There are usually a couple of guards inside, General. Do you think you can handle them alone?" Alabi asked.

Isoken scoffed as she wiped her flint-edged Kuname dagger with a handkerchief. "Be on the lookout," she said to them both. "Whenever I whistle, you rush in, grab your uncle and run as fast as you can. In the meantime, stay here and keep your eyes on the alleyways."

"General…" Alabi called. "After we save Uche, I want us to go after my father. He can assist you with your efforts."

Isoken grunted. She clamped the blade in her mouth and approached the workshop. The door creaked wide enough for her to slip through, and as soon as the door shut, there was an eerie silence. Alabi watched the workshop with Ruka, sweat forming on his back, every huff of breath sending chills down his spine. The air vibrated in the silence between them from the hum of the forge.

Within five minutes, they heard the general's signal—a sharp, piercing note that cut through the steam and above the thrum of machinery.

Ruka pointed with her chin. "Go." Her eyes scanned the rooftops.

"Find him and get out. I'll hold the alley." Alabi didn't argue; he slipped into the workshop as she turned back to face the street. When Alabi was inside, he ignored the wasteland of scattered, dismembered automatons and scanned through the exhausted huddle of people grovelling in a corner of the Forge. His eyes fell on Uche as Isoken stood next to the group, an imposing sentinel that caused the men to shrink and cower more at her presence.

"There," Alabi pointed. "Him."

Isoken lifted him by his arm and pulled him outside. Uche was too stunned to resist, his eyes wide as if he had seen an aether-striding masquerade.

As they returned to the alley, a strident, dissonant gong echoed throughout the city. Isoken, who was busy leading the way, stopped in her tracks. A quiver of fear coursed through Alabi's body as they halted.

"What's happening?" Ruka whispered, eyes darting around. They'd heard clanking sounds on a daily basis, but nothing as ear-piercing as this.

"They must know that we are here," Isoken said, snapping on her mask. "Whatever happens, stay close to me."

"Attention, people of Apapa and visitors," the tinny, emotionless voice came from the conical speakers mounted high under the eaves of each roof. "We are under attack. We urge you to stay calm as we deal with the situation. If, perhaps, you or a loved one gets killed in the chaos, consider it an act of patriotism. For the Queen Mother."

The ground quaked beneath their feet. Pebbles pranced on the cobblestones as automaton soldiers patrolled the entire city. The factory gates flew open, allowing scores of armoured heavy units to pass through, each of them holding incendiary cannons that expelled wild flames. Alabi, Ruka, and Uche looked to Isoken, awaiting her command, but all she said to them was "Run!"

They tore through the streets, running as fast as their legs could carry them. Automatons spotted them while they climbed toward the rooftop extraction point. As they mounted the roof, Alabi got his first clear look at the Cloud Maker—a monstrous airship, embattled with interlocking Kuname sheathing, emerging from the cloud layer. It was only when Isoken shouted her authorisation—and the automaton soldiers began spraying arcs of fire at them—that Alabi and the rest clambered hurriedly into the ship. The battleship lifted into the sky just as scores of automaton soldiers reached the roof with bursts of flames licking the underside of the hull.

"Shouldn't we go faster?" Alabi asked, his fingers twitching nervously with the hem of his buba.

"The ship is fortified with reinforced brass alloys," Isoken said, her voice calm as she checked a pressure gauge. "There's nothing to worry about."

Ruka threw herself into Alabi's arms, completely oblivious to her uncle's presence. Everything had happened in a breakneck, revving whir of accelerated moments. All their emotions had been compressed and stowed away, saddled under the tonnage of the mission, but at last, the pressure was lifting. It was the first moment they could finally, truly breathe, the air inside the vessel tasting of cool, filtered ozone instead of soot.

While Uche found his voice and began a low, urgent dialogue with Isoken, Ruka and Alabi wandered through the vibrating arteries and humming corridors of the ship, marvelling at the brass-bound logic of its pressurised design.

The airship lurched violently and swerved without warning, a rushing wind penetrating the windows. The pilot battled to stabilise the aircraft, his hands gripping white-knuckled as he wrestled to reign in the whirring rudder. Alabi staggered to the window, his gaze searching for the source of the sudden turbulence. His jaw dropped when he saw the ruby-eyed titan of brass and iron just beneath them, swinging a mighty hand in an attempt to swat the airship from the sky. The mechanatron had already rotated its massive, multi-barreled cannon, trained on the hull in preparation to fire.

"Uwa, get us out of here!" Isoken roared. "Everyone, brace for impact!"

"We're locked in the crosshairs!" Uwa shouted, frantically flipping a sequence of brass levers and clutching the rudder with every ounce of his strength.

Alabi was rooted to his spot by the window, overcome by paralysing wonder. When the giant pointed its weapon at the airship, it felt as though it were aiming for his very soul. As the pilot struggled to evade the cannon's trajectory, the giant suddenly paused. Billows of steam ejected in a thunderous, pressurised hiss from its back as the command cockpit opened, and a man revealed himself.

"Alabi!" Korede screamed, his voice strained with a desperate apprehension. "Alabi, is that you?!"

Alabi's heart skipped a beat as he stared at his father with widened eyes. If his father hadn't recognised him—if he hadn't been standing right by the glass porthole—he would have been vapourised. Just like that, his father would have murdered his own son in the name of progress. Alabi's chin trembled; he realised then how far his father had drifted into the machinery of the enemy. Was he truly willing to go all the way for this terrible, tyrannical cause?

Ruka pulled a rigid Alabi away from the window. He was still in shock when he saw a silhouette standing on the high balcony of a soot-stained spire. With coiling black tresses, a flowing velvet dress, and a body made of polished and ornate golden metal, the Queen Mother was every bit the garish, gilded mechanical deity Ruka had described. Ruka, Uche, and Isoken were riveted as well, their gazes fixed in a momentary trance of collective abhorrence as the airship regained its bearing and veered into the clouds.

The rest of the day was quiet except for the blustery howl

of wind, the rhythmic thrum of the engine, and the soft footsteps of Alabi as he observed the aircraft, gasping at its intricate clockwork architecture. In the corner, the quiet sobs from Uche echoed—a man who still couldn't believe he was finally within reach of saving his country. Ruka whispered words of comfort as she rubbed her uncle's back, her own tears tracing tracks through the soot on her cheeks.

Alabi soon settled on a spot near the viewing portal. The image of his father emerging from the brass maw of the giant played on a loop in his mind. For the first time since her death, Alabi called on Labake's spirit. "Help me," he mumbled, burying his head in his legs. "Help me save my people. Help me save my father from himself."

By the time it was dawn, the monumental, riveted walls of Benin were in sight, stretching across the horizon in an unshakeable promise. As the sun rose, Alabi's hope was rekindled. Isoken stood in their midst, arms folded behind her in a stance of grim pride.

"Here we are, folks," she said, as the Cloud Maker began its steady descent toward the sprawling city of bronze and greenery. "Welcome to the Benin Empire."

8

APRIL 26, 1866
BENIN EMPIRE, EDO-DELTA REGION

The Benin Empire resembled a vast, concentric maze, fortified by three massive walls of brick and Kuname. Above emanated an iridescent forcefield in a shimmering dome covering the entire city. A reverberating sound of rotating gears and shifting locks welcomed Alabi and the rest as an airship portal set in the titanic gates rumbled open.

The largest wall, at the outermost part of the empire, was a solid mass of steel and stone, spanning a staggering fifty metres in height. In between the largest and the middle walls were cylindrical houses of red clay, reinforced with oxidized brass and woven patterns of intricate embroidery amidst immaculate decorative metalwork. Nearly every household owned a horse-drawn cart and was surrounded by lush greenery, from decorative bushes and courtyard gardens, to farmlands, grazing grounds, and separate fields for rearing ostriches and horses. Clear streams flowed from the centre of the empire, spiralling into a brilliant blue lake where fishermen steered softly chugging steam-powered boats. There was an industrial sector at the far edge of the empire, where filtered huffs of steam diffused through the pristine blue sky.

The people of Benin, clad in vibrant red wrappers and polished clay beads, went about their day without noticing the airship passing by. They seemed like carefree people who had never known war or the frigid shackle of the Queen's iron in their lives.

The Oba's palace, about fifty feet tall, stood at the centre and was the largest structure within the kingdom's walls. It was built like a majestic monument, with inner courtyards and walls etched in relief or adorned with bronze statues of past kings. Their history and ancestry watched over the entire city with unblinking eyes. The airship didn't fly towards the palace; instead, it landed at a nearby sprawling mansion.

"We aren't going to see the oba?" Ruka asked, her voice hushed as she took in the scale of the interior.

"The Oba of Benin is a divine entity. He does not reveal himself until there are matters that threaten the very soul of the empire," Isoken explained, her tone bordering on a warning.

"But this is serious, General. The Queen Mother and her automaton soldiers could infiltrate your empire and siphon the very life from it, just like Apapa—just like Itu Atan," Alabi said, his eyes wide with urgency.

"Chief Irabor maintains that our fortifications are absolute, so he doesn't expect this matter to disturb His Majesty," Isoken said. A slight trace of frustration tightened her jaw.

Uche was the only one who didn't utter a word. He'd been ruminating throughout the journey, undoubtedly calculating the tensile strength of the automatons and devising ways to overpower them to forge a path toward independence.

Isoken led the way to Chief Irabor's front door, where two armed soldiers guarded the entrance, their Kuname-plated armour gleaming.

"The Chief has summoned us," Isoken told the guards, her steely eyes daring them to impede her progress. One of the soldiers struck his ceremonial staff against the stone and motioned to Alabi, Ruka, and Uche.

"Turn out your pockets," Isoken said with a sigh, and they immediately complied. Alabi submitted his brass-rimmed binoculars, and Uche presented a jagged shard of industrial steel he had kept from the Forge. Ruka seemingly had nothing on her, but Alabi recalled the lethal weight of the dagger she had carried earlier. He wondered what shadow she had tucked it into.

With a nod of agreement, the soldiers let them pass, but their unblinking gazes followed the outsiders as they walked. Chief Irabor's home was a bastion suited for a man of war. The walls were encrusted with relief sculptures of valiant ironclad warriors armed with spears, shields, and swords. Alabi examined the terracotta and bronze sculptures, noting that one of them bore a striking resemblance to Isoken—as if her lineage was etched into the very masonry and metalwork.

Before long, Chief Irabor emerged. He looked to be about sixty years old, with a slightly creased face and a bushy grey beard. His body, however, remained formidable—broad and chiselled, his muscles straining under his blinding white singlet. The chief strutted in, an aura of vested nobility and martial power surrounding his stride. As if on cue, Alabi, Ruka, and Uche bowed before him. Isoken maintained her stoic composure, offering a swift, respectful bow as he drew near.

"I didn't expect to see three people," he said in a stentorian voice that seemed to vibrate the floor.

"There was a slight change in plans, and I had to bring them with me," Isoken replied, her voice steady.

"Hmm," Chief Irabor said, his sharp eyes dissecting the three guests who bowed low before him. "Get up."

They straightened, each shaking off the tension of the bow.

Chief Irabor assessed Ruka, his eyes narrowing with precision."What's your name, child?"

"Ruka," she said. Her eyes met the chief's gaze, a look of strength and resolve that deepened her reply.

"This one will make a great fighter," he said, a knowing smile creasing his weathered face. "I can see it in her form."

Uche instantly became uneasy. Beads of sweat formed on his forehead, glistening in the lamplight. "Great Chief, my niece is only a teenager. She is not built for the life of a soldier."

Chief Irabor laughed, his voice a deep, cultured roar. "I used to think that way of my daughter, too, until she…" He motioned to Isoken. "…proved me wrong. She now commands my strongest division."

Isoken maintained her poise, unmoved by her father's flattery—or perhaps, beneath that mask, there was a tinge of pride and gratitude. Looking between Chief Irabor and Isoken, Alabi noticed the resemblance was more than skin deep. They had the same steely gaze and the same regal gait. Isoken was the tempered blade to Irabor's heavy hammer—a version that would surpass his many achievements.

Chief Irabor diverted his eyes to Alabi, the warmth vanishing instantly. "I assume you're the one who informed us of the intended attack."

Alabi nodded, swallowing hard. "Yes, sir. I believe they're planning something unprecedented."

Chief Irabor stroked his coarse beard, his expression turning inscrutable. "General Isoken, let us speak in private," he commanded, turning toward a heavy, bronze-reinforced door.

“What did you find out, Isoken?” The chief’s voice was a low, private rumble.

“Many things, Chief. The Queen Mother has absorbed a great number of the surrounding cities into her industrial machine. And the factory in the Niger Delta—the one we mocked for churning out rusted scrap—is rumoured to house unprecedented war technology, powerful enough to shatter our walls.”

Chief Irabor scoffed, the sound sharp and dismissive. “Impossible.”

“I saw the giant automaton with my own eyes, Father. And like you, I was certain that their machines could not touch us—but, Father, my overconfidence nearly cost me my life yesterday. I wouldn’t be standing before you if it weren’t for Alabi. I know we have never been conquered. I know that we possess the most resilient alloys and the most skilled warriors. I know that our wall is the mightiest fortification in all of history, but we mustn’t let pride become our downfall.”

Chief Irabor pondered Isoken’s words, his fingers tracing the deep scars on his knuckles. “What do you think we should do?”

“We have to mobilise the full strength of the guard

immediately. I sense the Queen Mother is already tightening the noose. They might try to ambush us within the next few days."

"Relax, Isoken. Our walls haven't been breached in centuries," Chief Irabor said, his voice thick with certainty. "We have never lost a war. Whatever happens, we will fight and we will win."

A brass-plated communicator on a nearby centre table emitted a sharp, pulsing chime, and Isoken answered. "Speak."

Her brows furrowed as she listened to the static-laced report.

"What's wrong?" the chief asked, his temples creasing as the first cracks of doubt appeared in his expression. Isoken looked at him, her face a mask of cold clarity. "They're here."

Isoken burst out of the room. "They're here!" she repeated to the guards in the hall.

She dashed out, whistled for a horse, and galloped towards the nearest watchtower. On reaching it, she dismounted and climbed into the mechanical, steam-driven lift, wrenching the levers so she could go faster. As soon as she reached the top, she took out her gold-rimmed monocular and looked ahead. A dry, bitter laugh escaped her lips.

"Centuries of peace," she spat, watching the horizon darken. "And it ends on the day of a full moon. The machines are ahead of schedule, and they came to see if our myths bleed."

Uche and Alabi scurried towards General Isoken when she re-entered the mansion, her face tightening in determination.

"How many are they?" Uche asked. His voice was tight with the familiar anxiety of the hunted.

"About a thousand; calvary riding on clockwork horses and at least two giant mechanatrons. They should reach us by late morning. There's no sign of an airship, which is quite intriguing, since their last attempted incursion was an aerial assault." She paused in thought. "I need to discern the shape of their shadow before it falls on us."

Isoken strode past them, to where her father was. On her way, she met Ruka who said, "General, I want to be among the fighters. I can hold a line."

Isoken let out a grunt and brushed Ruka off impulsively with the blunt force of a woman already at war. "Get out of my way, child. This isn't a skirmish in an alley; it's an extinction, should we fail."

Ruka watched in desperation as Isoken strode ahead.

"Be patient, Ruka," Alabi said, glancing over her shoulder.

Alabi's heart raced. His father was most likely embedded in that marching army. Korede might have been many things, but he had never been a warrior—certainly not one forged to survive a clash of empires. Alabi was no soldier either, but for the sake of the blood still in his veins and the people behind these walls, he would stand and fight. He pressed his eyes shut and prayed to his mother, trusting that her spirit would guide them.

Isoken re-emerged, already buckling an ornate bronze-colored breastplate over her uniform. "Prepare the horses," she told the servants, and like leaves in a gale, they quickly dispersed.

"Uche," Isoken called, her gaze pinning him to the spot. "I understand you have led a resistance for years. You know how these machines fail. Chief Irabor and I need your expertise if we are going to break this siege."

Uche nodded in accordance, his chest raised in pride, as if he had been consecrated for a holy duty. He had waited nine years for this opportunity. Turning to Ruka and Alabi, Isoken said, "Are you sure you want to step into this fire? You could remain within these walls, and when the smoke clears, you can tell us what we need to know."

"I want to fight," Ruka said through a clenched jaw set like a hardened flint.

"Ruka, you don't have anything to prove," Uche said. The desperation in his voice carried through the hall.

"No, Uncle. I have to do this. Alabi and I will fight," Ruka replied, not flinching from his gaze.

"Alabi, please, reason with her," Uche begged. "I wouldn't want to lose her like I lost her mother."

"You won't lose her," Alabi said. "I have seen Ruka show the kind of bravery that can't be taught. She is a valiant warrior, one forged in the shadow of the Queen Mother herself."

Uche let out a sigh of resignation, his shoulders slumping under the weight of his fear. Then, he took a step forward and placed a heavy, calloused hand on Ruka, pulling her into the circle of his protection one last time.

"If you must go, then go with the strength of our ancestors," he whispered, looking between them, his eyes gleaming with a fierce pride. "I will see you when the sun sets on a free land."

Isoken looked at them for a moment, waiting for someone to object, searching for a hint of hesitation. When she found none, she said, "Okay then. Come with me, Uche. I will order the servants to take both of you to the Great Armoury first, then to the lower courtyard where the vanguard is gathering. Return with honour."

Alabi and Ruka were hurriedly led to the armoury, a cavernous chamber that smelled of oil, cold bronze, and ancient soot. A smith, whose arms seemed as thick as the beams used for the city gates, sized them up with a grunt. He tossed a breastplate and helmet of Kuname-reinforced brass to Alabi and a flexible crimson leather tunic studded with copper to Ruka.

"Don't expect them to feel like a second skin," the smith growled. "They are meant to keep you alive, not comfortable."

Alabi fumbled with the straps, his fingers trembling. He felt the weight of the metal pressing against his chest, a physical manifestation of the choice he had made. Ruka, however, strapped her gear on with a grim efficiency. She reached into a crate and pulled out a Kuname short sword, testing its balance.

"You look like a soldier," Alabi whispered.

"I look like someone who is tired of running," she replied, her voice steady and reassuring.

They followed a servant to the courtyard that served as the vanguard's training grounds, where a battalion of soldiers was lined up in terrifyingly precise formations. The air was thick with the mechanical groan of heavy machinery and the metallic tang of sharpening blades. The empire had found a way to evacuate those living in the outer rings—a tactical manoeuvre suggested by Uche, which Chief Irabor had reluctantly authorised.

Warships were stationed in the training area, hissing with built-up pressure near a herd of armoured horses whose plates clattered with every restless hoofbeat. The soldiers manned the heavy-bore cannon guns fixed to the battlements' embrasures to secure the height advantage. Near the arrow slits, archers took their positions, their eyes fixed on the distant dust clouds of the encroaching enemy.

The soldiers in the watchtower, armed and observant, made sure to relay every shift in the approaching tide back to Isoken. Within a half hour, the entire empire was humming with the vibration of a city turning into a fortress.

The people were agitated, but their faith remained tempered by history; they trusted in the lethal competence of Isoken and the army of Irabor—the same army that had been undefeated for decades.

General Isoken ordered Ruka to stay on one of the scout ships. Uche had pleaded for his niece to be given the least dangerous duty, and patrolling the skies seemed the best fit. Alabi, however, was positioned on the Benin wall at the primary ramparts to fight from above. His bronze-lined breastplate and helmet weighed on him, but he felt a surging heat of pride as he gripped a Kuname blade, its edge shimmering with a strange, iridescent light. He had dismantled an automaton once in his hometown; he was certain he could destroy many more. His only prayer was that the spirits would shield those he cared for from the coming fire.

Isoken emerged at the front of the army. She, too, was clad in helmet and breastplate, but hers bore the intricate scrollwork of imperial distinction, the Great Bronze Mask symbol gleaming in the morning sun. Her voice rose over the industrial roar of the encroaching army.

"Warriors of Great Benin!"

"Eh!" they thundered, the sound rattling the stones of

the courtyard.

"The mighty descendants of Ozolua!"

"Eh!"

"For decades, we have held our place in this nation. We have conquered territories and have erected the most impenetrable walls in the world! To protect our heritage and preserve our histories, we severed our ties to the outside world. Since that day, we have been a constant target for those who desire to strip our wealth and exploit our genius. Today, they have come again—not as men, but as cogs in a soulless machine!"

"Ehhh!"

"But a machine has no heart! A machine has no ancestors to answer to! We are the wall that has never broken! We have just one mission: to grind the invaders into dust!"

"Ehhh!"

"Tear those automatons apart!"

"Ehhh!"

A tremendous roar went up from the soldiers, a sound so loud it felt like it could shake the very clouds. The amber-citrine sky of the morning was choked by a rising wall of grey dust. The clockwork army was close—the rhythmic, shuddering thud of their mechanical strides vibrating through the earth.

"Make them wish they never stepped foot on our territory! We go in the name of the Oba and the spirits of Benin!"

The soldiers let out a booming roar as they mounted

their horses and cantered towards the battlefield. The walls rumbled open, allowing the passage of about two hundred of Benin's fiercest warriors. Isoken surveyed the area from the front lines. Four monstrous mechanatron giants led the attack—awful marvels of sinister technology cast in silhouette against the distant mountains. Behind them marched a battalion of automaton ground units, a rhythmic, terrifying *clack-clack-clack* that sounded like the heartbeat of an angry god.

The automatons wielded long-range rifles and flamethrowers, but their greatest advantage lay in the four colossi. Alabi looked between the four monstrosities, wondering in which iron ribcage his father was trapped. He had barely begun to guess when Isoken screamed, "Attack!"

The first row of Benin soldiers had positioned towering sonic war drums in front of them. At Isoken's command, they struck the stretched leather with a rhythmic fury, sending out distorting sonic waves that peeled back the metallic topcoats of the lead automatons. The ones who couldn't hold their stance were flung backward, crashing into their own ranks and setting off a tumbling, grinding chain of destruction.

Benin fired the cannons, launching glowing spherical projectiles made of pure Kuname metal towards the giants. Even with each cannon's powerful momentum, the mechanatrons only staggered, their heavy pistons hissing in complaint as they stabilised. The soldiers fired again and again until a cannonball ripped through the brass plating of the lead mechanatron, shredding its exterior to reveal a wounded man slumped inside the cockpit.

A cloud of dust shrouded the Benin warriors as the automaton troops charged, their clockwork horses advancing with mechanically actuated agility, each stride cratering large footprints into the ground. Once they were within combat range, the horses' heads reconfigured—plates sliding back to reveal integrated barrels—to shoot bullets the size of pebbles that whistled through the air like a flurry of hail.

The Benin warriors raised their shields, but the sheer kinetic force of the blasts sent soldiers flying across the field.

"Watch out for those mounts!" Isoken bellowed, her Kuname blade a blur as she sliced through a clockwork horse, severing the sparking pistons and synthetic tendons in its neck. She moved with lethal quickness, a whirlwind of slashing and dodging. Her soldiers followed suit, replicating the fluid, high-stakes techniques she had drilled into them.

Alabi, for a minute, was transfixed. There he was, the son of an inventor, witnessing a mechanical apocalypse unfold. And although a part of him worried for his father, he felt a greater sense of responsibility—a debt to Imade, to his mother, and to the very soil of his country. Alabi loaded the cannonballs, watching as they rammed into the advancing steel line with bone-shattering impact.

"Target the power cores in their chests and the exhaust tubes in their backs!" Alabi shouted. The archers responded instantly, raining down hundreds of arrows, many of them wedging into the delicate vents of the automaton soldiers.

All of a sudden, a grenade landed a few feet away from Alabi with a soft, sickening thud. Before he could react, it exploded. The impact hurled him into the air, slamming him against the wall's edge. Alabi slipped from the brink, his helmet clattering away as he tumbled toward the chaos below. A soldier lunged, grabbing his arm, but the secondary shockwave of a cannon blast broke their hold.

Slowly—too slowly—Alabi fell. Mid-air, his adrenaline surged, reestablishing a desperate urgency. Wind screamed in his ears as he searched for a lifeline. His fingers caught a looped rope, the friction burning his palms, as a sharp pain bloomed in his chest. Warm blood gushed from a gash on his forehead. As bullets whipped around him, the soldiers on the wall threw down two more ropes and hauled him back up. Amidst the exchange of gunfire, Alabi was steadied back on his feet. He was stunned and injured, but he was alive.

The ground beneath them rumbled, groaned, and heaved.

"Stay alert!" Isoken cried, her voice cutting through the din. "Keep your eyes open!" Her soldiers looked around frantically, fear and confusion clouding their discipline.

Behind them, the ground closest to the outer wall suddenly cracked, then shattered, unveiling a fifth colossal mechanatron—a subterranean predator born of industrial malice, rising up from the depths.

They pivoted the emplacements and fired every charge they had, but the realisation came too late: the ground wasn't just shaking; it was hollow. Two more giants erupted from the fractured earth inside the outer wall, followed by a tidal wave of armoured automaton soldiers. They ignored the perimeter, carving a path toward the heart of the city while dodging the cannonballs and desperate hail of arrows.

Among the five giants lumbered a gargantuan golden frame, crafted with a regal, terrifying precision. Its fine brass skeleton was reinforced with thick, interlocking sheathing that gleamed with an aura of inevitability. *The Queen Mother*, Alabi thought, his breath hitching. She wasn't merely leading the army; she was the engine of doom at its centre.

Looking up, Alabi noticed the Benin airship carrying Ruka was descending to retrieve Isoken. He signaled frantically as the vessel began to reascend into the smoke-choked air, and grabbed onto the reinforced rope that Isoken was climbing. His muscles strained as he was hauled upwards.

"We have to pursue the breach," Isoken said, her boots hitting the deck of the airship with a heavy thud. She let out a short, stilted laugh that held no humour. "Tunnels…

they burrowed beneath our very feet? I must admit, I am impressed by such a calculated insult."

"What's the plan, General? If they reach the inner circle, the empire falls," Ruka said as she white-knuckled the ship's railing.

"They won't," Isoken said, her eyes darting across the tactical display. "My veterans have fortified the interior of the second wall. They're positioned for an ambush that will turn these narrow streets into an automaton graveyard. We still hold the heavens; our airships are our greatest advantage."

"But the civilians?" Alabi asked, his voice cracking over the roar of a distant explosion. "The families caught between the rings—what becomes of them when the automaton reaches their doors?"

"We will protect them at all costs," Isoken said, but Alabi sensed the hollow ring in her resolve. The Benin high command had been blinded by their own history; they had never prepared for a war that burrowed beneath their feet. Every time the automatons deployed a new articulated joint or a high-pressure steam vent, Alabi saw the ghost of his father's genius—the exact mechanical curves he had seen sketched in the soot on their backyard wall.

"I'm not staying in the clouds while the city burns," Ruka said, checking the tension on her hidden blade. "I'm going after the golden one. I'm going after the Queen Mother."

"I'm with you," Alabi said, his fear eclipsed by a cold, desperate need for answers.

They performed a low-altitude drop at the inner ramparts, landing amidst the deafening thunder of cannon fire and harpoons. Soldiers were raining projectiles mercilessly upon the invaders, but the Golden Giant moved with a haughty, terrifying grace. It stepped into the line of fire, acting as a living bulwark; the heavy Kuname harpoons simply sparked and skittered off its reinforced frame without leaving a single dent on its frame.

"Keep firing!" Isoken yelled. She strained as she watched their most powerful munitions fail. "Don't let that golden monster take another step!"

Ruka had her eyes fixed on the golden giant, her focus so absolute that she broke into a sprint toward it.

"Focus on the foot soldiers!" Isoken bellowed from somewhere across the smoke. "Leave the giants to the artillery!" Ruka turned, her lips pulled back in a feral snarl, but she obeyed and veered away from her charge. She had lashed her dagger to a weighted staff, swinging it in lethal, sweeping arcs. Her movements were a dance—the staff a fluid extension of her will, keeping time to a noiseless rhythm amidst the chaos.

On the ramparts, the archers had swapped their bows for pneumatic magnetic harpoons. Each discharge hissed and hummed as it pierced through the automatons' hulls, unleashing high-frequency shockwaves that shattered internal circuits and left the machines twitching in the dirt before falling inert.

Alabi scanned around for anything that could propel him upward. He needed to mount the golden giant; he had to find the access seal to force the cockpit open. He spotted a pyramid-shaped building nearby, its mud-brick walls reinforced with protruding wooden torons, and began to climb.

The second giant, still lurking in the shadow of its golden protector, tracked Alabi's ascent. With a groan of stressed metal, it swung a massive limb to collapse the structure beneath him. Alabi split his focus, manoeuvring to dodge attacks and calculating how to clear the yawning gap between the crumbling masonry and the giant's shoulder. He needed a leap of pure momentum, or he would be crushed by the very building he scaled.

"Alabi!" Ruka screamed.

As soon as the words left her mouth, the building gave way with a deafening crack, and Alabi instinctively leapt. He felt suspended in the air, a heartbeat of weightlessness before he landed roughly on the engraved torso of the golden giant. The impact forced a spray of copper-tasting blood from his lips.

The golden giant bucked, trying to wriggle him off like a flea, but he held on with white-knuckled ferocity. The other giant—the one that had razed the building—levelled a flamethrower at him. Alabi dived into a narrow crevice between the golden plates, his armour acting as a heat shield as a torrent of fire roared past. Alabi could feel the blistering radiation on his back, heard Ruka's muffled screams over the thundering percussion of the cannons.

Then, the golden mechanatron pivoted.

To Alabi's shock, it raised its arm and fired a compressed kinetic blast at its own ally, sending the other giant reeling backward into a storm of Benin cannon fire. With a slow, deliberate motion, the golden mechanatron extracted Alabi from the crevice in its torso and placed him gently on the ground beside an ashen-faced, thunderstruck Ruka.

It then lunged at the other giant, its fists moving with piston-driven fury. It punched repeatedly until its knuckles formed a deep, shattered depression that that deformed the machine's core. In a final motion, the golden giant gripped the head of its fallen comrade, wrenching it clear in a spray of sparks and steam, before plucking out the terrified driver within.

Alabi, dazed and wounded, watched in a state of fractured confusion as the golden mechanatron shuddered. A series of pneumatic hisses echoed through the courtyard as the torso retracted, expelling a thick, humid plume of steam from its inner sanctum.

Korede slipped out of the cockpit, stumbling as his feet hit the blood-soaked earth. Ruka moved with the speed of a striking viper, brandishing her staff-blade at his throat. She stopped just short of a killing blow only when she saw Korede's eyes—rimmed with a desperate, bloodshot red, his knees trembling under a weight that wasn't purely mechanical. He collapsed beside his son, his breath coming in ragged gasps.

"I can't… I cannot do it anymore," Korede whispered, the words dissolving into gut-wrenching sobs that seemed to rattle his very bones. Alabi's face was a contradictory mosaic of pain and pity, of confusion and cold fury, of worry and shame. Tears tracked through the dust and bruises on his cheeks. He was profoundly grateful that his father lived, that he had relented, yet he felt the violent urge to punch him for the chaos he had steered.

Benin guards swarmed Korede, pinioning his arms and fastening heavy brass manacles about his wrists. Alabi watched, anchored by his own injuries, as the man who had built his world was treated like a common criminal

Before the guards could haul him away, Ruka stepped into Korede's line of sight, her brows fused together in a tight, unforgiving grimace. "Where is she?" she demanded, the edge of her blade still glinting. "Where's the Queen Mother?"

"She is headed for the palace," Korede said, his head bowed low, the golden light of the mechanatron casting a mocking halo over his regret.

Ruka shook her head, her voice thick with disbelief. "Impossible. We are dismantling your vanguard. No machine could have slipped past the General's line unnoticed."

Korede met her amber eyes, his voice an exasperated rasp. "She is no automaton, child. The Queen Mother is human, and she is already inside."

Ruka and Alabi exchanged petrified looks, their gazes snapping toward the distant silhouette of the Oba's palace.

"The palace is a fortress; it is the most heavily guarded structure in the empire," Alabi said, trying to convince himself as much as Ruka. "Assuming she is human… she has a way in we haven't seen. We must stay alert." Ruka nodded.

As the guards began to drag Korede toward the holding cells, he dug his heels into the dirt. "Wait! There is something else…"

Alabi tensed. "What is it, Bàámì?"

"The Queen Mother's plan was never a simple siege, Alabi. She used the army as a distraction—a loud, iron mask to hide her true movement. She has slipped through the fractured walls to plant thermic-resonant bombs. Her goal isn't just to conquer; she wants the formula for Kuname. Once she cripples the city, she will harvest its secrets to forge a tide of indestructible machinery that no nation can ever hope to halt."

"Where are they, Bàámì? Tell us where she placed them!" Alabi cried, reaching out as his father was pulled back.

"She didn't trust me with the exact locations," Korede shouted, his heels carving deep furrows in the red earth. "But she uses aether-triggers—look for the shimmering blue heat-haze near the palace vents and its reservoir. You have to hurry; once the timers are primed, you have only four minutes before the centre of the city becomes a tomb of molten glass. Go! Stop her! Save the heart of Benin before she silences it forever!"

"Search the empire!" Isoken screamed, her eyes red with rage. "Find that woman!"

The plan was to split up, but the moment their boots hit the palace stone, Ruka ignited. She bolted ahead, a vivid streak of red outstripping the platoon of soldiers assigned to the hunt. The guards stationed at the grand entrance lay dead, struck down by their own ceremonial weapons—a cruel efficiency that only a master of the craft could execute. Ruka leapt over the fallen, her shadow flickering against the regal chambers.

The palace felt eerie and hollow, as if the very air had been vacuumed out. The Oba and his retinue had retreated to the subterranean sanctums. She checked the gardens, the corridors, and ended up in one of the courtyards. Ruka sidestepped an overturned lampstand, tracing a glistening trail of arterial red that led up the grand staircase and toward the high throne room. From behind the heavy timber doors, she heard laboured, wet breathing and soft, rhythmic groans of the dying. She gripped her blade, her pulse a hammer-strike in her ears, and swallowed before carefully using her boot to nudge the door open.

She edged into the grand chamber. To her left, she found her Uncle Uche slumped, his form shattered and soaked in crimson. Ruka crouched beside him, tears streaming down her cheeks and blurring her vision as her trembling hands hovered over his chest, hesitant to touch. She wiped her eyes with a savage motion and turned toward the woman whose back was to them—a figure who watched the empty throne with unnerving, unmoving stupefaction. Ruka moved with silent precision, snatching an ornamental staff to bolt the massive doors, sealing them inside.

"He is alive; you should take him to your healers," the Queen Mother said, her voice as smooth and cold as polished glass. Her black pigtails drifted in the steady wind whistling through the high rafters.

"Let me see your face!" Ruka spat, her voice thick with a cobra's venom.

The Queen Mother swivelled, revealing a delicate, freckled face and enchanting purple eyes that held a fragmented light. It was her right arm, however, that commanded Ruka's attention: from her shoulder blade to her fingertips, the flesh had been replaced with a golden mechanical appendage, a complex lattice of hissing micro-pistons and engraved brass plating that caught the dim light like a dying star.

"The line of the Oba has reached its inevitable end. Benin shall behold its new sovereign—the Queen Mother—and the name Merritt shall be whispered with awe across a borderless empire!" She turned to Ruka, a sneer twisting her freckled features as she raised her gauntleted arm, a masterpiece of sleek, vicious technological craft. "You come from the soot of Apapa, child. You have spent your life kneeling in the dirt I provided. Why stop now, when you can finally bow to a goddess of your own making?"

"You are going to pay for what you did to my uncle!" Ruka retorted, her clenched knuckles cracking as she gripped her blade with furious disdain. She lunged, slashing at the Queen Mother with a desperate speed. The Kuname dagger clashed against the woman's mechanical elbow, a deafening, crystalline clang echoing throughout the vaulted chamber.

Ruka pivoted fluidly in response and swept the dagger toward the Queen Mother's throat, but her opponent moved with inhuman precision. She deftly sidestepped the arc, her left hand clamping onto Ruka's wrist like a vice of cold flesh, while her golden right arm drove a shattering punch into Ruka's gut.

Despite her reinforced armour, the concussive force sent

a spray of blood from Ruka's lips. The world tilted into a sickening spin as she tried in vain to steady herself. Before she could find her footing, the Queen Mother struck again and again—each piston-driven blow lifting Ruka off the ground until she finally collapsed, folding into a shattered heap against the stone.

On the other side of the heavy timber, Alabi, Isoken, and her soldiers were thundering against the door, the wood groaning under the weight of their ram. Ruka's vision blurred through a haze of tears and copper-tasting blood, but she could see the Queen Mother towering over her, before the woman turned away to behold the throne room with a chillingly vacant stare.

Ruka had one last trick remaining—a final spark of defiance before the darkness claimed her. She detonated her smoke bomb, and the room was instantly swallowed by a dense, acrid cloud of royal purple. Queen Merritt covered her nostrils, her mechanical arm raised in a defensive guard as she searched the shifting mist.

The throne room door finally splintered and burst open just as Ruka levelled her sidearm. She fired three shots through the haze, the muzzle flashes illuminating the purple gloom. She emerged from the mist, her finger tightening for a fourth, when Alabi caught her from behind, pulling her into a stifling embrace.

"That's enough," Alabi shouted, his voice raw. "We need her alive—we need the codes!"

They both stared at the Queen. The bullets were flattened and embedded in shallow depressions on her breastplate, having failed to pierce her stolen Kuname armour. Isoken lunged forward, tackling the monarch to the ground and binding her wrists with heavy, resonance-dampening cuffs. The Queen Mother offered no resistance, her gaze fixed on Ruka.

"You're a good fighter," Queen Merritt quipped to Ruka, her entire demeanour still unbroken and unbowed. Exhausted and spent, blood trickled from the edges of Ruka's open mouth. She wavered and finally slumped into Alabi's arms, the silence of the palace returning as the purple smoke began to clear.

"Where are the bombs?" Isoken asked through clenched teeth, her fingers knotted in Queen Merritt's hair as she violently jerked her head back.

The woman fixed a piercing purple gaze at Isoken and began to laugh. The sound was cold, shrill, and metallic, bouncing off the marble walls and spiralling into the high-arched ceilings.

"Surrender your empire and I will halt the sequence. All I need is to issue one vocal command to stop the timers."

Isoken tightened her grip, the veins in her knuckles

bulging. "And if we refuse?"

"Then you watch your legacy crumble, and your people die in the ruins."

A heavy silence descended, broken only by the ragged, laboured breathing of Uche and Ruka, and the mournful whistle of the wind gently billowing through the silk drapery in the rafters. With her free hand, Isoken unsheathed her Kuname dagger, the blade shimmering with cold promise as she pressed it against the Queen's throat.

"Kill me if you wish, but understand this: I am merely the first gear in a grander engine." Merritt's voice was unshaken and steady.

"What do you mean?" Isoken hissed, the blade drawing a bead of crimson.

"I have set forces in motion that cannot be reversed. The people believe in the order I've built, even though they fear it. Power is a magnetic force; it will always attract those hungry enough to continue my design. Even this great empire that many have tried to conquer, which you guard so jealously…" The Queen Mother scanned the throne room with a clinical, detached gaze.

"The Benin Empire was not built on a single dream. It was a slow, brutal progression. Do you think this glory rose without the grinding of bone or the shedding of blood? Humanity, as it stands, is weak—frail, emotional, and dangerously unpredictable. Someone must impose order; someone must forge a future from metal and steam. If I fall today, you merely make me a martyr, and another will rise from the clinkers of my ashes."

In a flash of revulsion, Isoken struck Merritt across the jaw with the heavy bronze pommel of her dagger. She watched with a grim satisfaction as blood coursed down the woman's lips, yet the Queen Mother's mouth merely curled into a menacing, fragmented grin.

The Queen Mother spat a glob of blood onto the pristine floor and whispered, "You had better hurry, General. *Tick-tock. Tick-tock.*"

"Quickly, haul her to the dungeon!" Isoken commanded, her voice cutting through the rising panic as she hurried away to the balustrades overlooking the city. To the remaining men, she yelled, "Clear the inner rings! Get as many folks as possible to the safe houses near the outer fortifications!"

Alabi supported a staggering, injured Ruka while a few soldiers hoisted Uche's limp form hastily from the throne room. Outside, a Benin airship hovered, its steam-vents hissing as it waited to whisk them away from the epicenter of the coming blast.

"I have to go—I have to help the people," Alabi whispered to Ruka. His eyes scanned the smoke-veiled, war-torn cityscape. He saw the shimmering heat-haze his father had warned him about, ghostly blue distortions rising near the palace vents below.

Ruka gave a faint nod of understanding, leaning her

weight against him and resting her head on his shoulder for a fleeting, fragile moment. "Promise me you will come back," she said.

Alabi pressed a brief, fierce kiss to her forehead. "I promise."

The sanctuary of the empire had transformed into a frenzied bottleneck, hundreds of people scrambling to safety as they poured through the reinforced thresholds of the subterranean safe houses.

Isoken rushed to Alabi, her face smeared with soot and resolve. "The sonic grenades are primed and on a timer." Her voice was barely audible over the cacophony of the panic. Alabi leaned in close so Isoken could put her lips to his ear. "You have less than four minutes to detonate them at the structural nodes and find cover. I have etched the coordinates onto this map." She paused, placing a heavy hand on his shoulder, her gaze burning with a rare, solemn respect. "Thank you, Alabi, for doing this. The Benin Empire will remain forever indebted to you for your sacrifice."

She handed him a pair of brass-fitted ear protectors, lined with thick wool. "May the gods of our ancestors guide your hand."

Earlier…

"I sent word to our Royal Guild of Inventors the moment I heard of the bombs," Isoken had told Ruka and Alabi as they soared to the palace. "In case we fail to capture the Queen Mother, or if she proves too stubborn to confess, we have devised a method to triangulate the aetheric signature of the explosives. The plan is to station sonic grenades at the primary structural nodes. She likely targeted the load-bearing pillars—the points that will yield the most catastrophic collapse. She may have studied our palace from afar, but she cannot navigate its inner masonry as well as we can.

"Our inventors have been developing and refining these sonic grenades for many seasons, but they have never been tempered in the fires of actual war," Isoken continued. "Our best hope is to trigger the grenades seconds before the Queen Mother's bombs detonate. We can only know how long we have once someone gets close enough to an explosive to determine the timing. The counter-vibration should, in theory, neutralise the blast. To achieve that, we need a volunteer to be within the detonation radius to prime the sonic cores."

"Would that work?" Ruka asked.

"We are treading on unproven physics," Isoken admitted.

"How can you know if the resonance will even hold?" Ruka asked, her voice tight with doubt.

"It is the only gamble we have left."

"I'll do it," Alabi said, his voice steady, earning him startled glances from both Ruka and Isoken. "But we must find and secure the Queen Mother as well. We need to know the countdown. I have raced against a ticking clock before; I can do it again."

The safe house was filling up fast to capacity. Like the Queen Mother's bombs, the sonic grenades were instruments of violent physics; regardless of which force won, the populace needed to be shielded beneath the earth.

Two minutes…

Alabi unveiled the final explosive, readying to place the last sonic grenade at its designated nexus. He cast a desperate glance toward the stone well beside him, calculating the distance and praying his reflexes would be swift enough to carry him into its depths.

One minute…

His fingers trembled, the brass casing of the grenade slick with his perspiration. Sweat poured down his face, stinging his eyes as he struggled to maintain his composure. He rehearsed the sequence in a frantic whisper, a mantra of survival against the looming shadow of the clock.

Thirty seconds…

Ten seconds…

Five…

At the five-second mark, Alabi triggered the sonic core as he tossed the grenade at the base of the planted bomb. He threw himself into the well and hauled the heavy lid shut just as the atmosphere outside fractured.

An ear-splitting shriek and three thunderous detonations erupted in a singular, devastating moment. The clash of opposing frequencies set off a seismic chain reaction that rattled the empire to its very foundations. Every pane of glass in the city shattered into a million diamond-like shards; loose objects were repelled by the kinetic shockwave as if by an invisible hand. The ground groaned as buildings cracked and succumbed underneath the tension, the earth opening in spiderwebbing crevices. Even the legendary great walls were damaged, bits of protective sheathing stripped away to reveal their skeletal Kuname scaffolding of thick rods that alone prevented total collapse.

The primary tremors had only just subsided when the airships began their staccato descent. The people emerged from the safe houses in the settling aftermath of the blast, gasping at the warped landscape of their home.

Ruka sprinted toward the well, her breath coming in ragged stitches, but found it empty, the lid cast aside. She searched the stream, then the meadow where a smattering of livestock lay in ghastly repose, blood trickling from their ears and mouths from the devastating sonic pressure of the shockwaves. She scrambled past overturned carts and the splintered ruins of dwellings, coming to a stop beside the corpse of a man felled from the shock. Her heart pounded with dread when Alabi remained nowhere to be found.

The crackle of twigs behind her snapped her focus, and she whipped around, her blade already half-drawn. The breath left her lungs when she saw it was him.

Alabi emerged from the settling grit, his face masked in a thick layer of grey dust and soot.

Tears spilled down her cheeks, carving tracks through the grime on her own face, as she collided with him. She threw her arms around him, clinging to him with a feral intensity until she could feel the steady, thundering rhythm of his heartbeat against her own. Alabi held her just as tightly, his hand supporting the small of her back as he pulled her in for a kiss that tasted of copper, ash, and an impossible relief.

9

Horns sounded as royal messengers galloped through the debris, alerting every nobleman to an emergency council at the palace. The devastation was absolute: half the dwellings within the inner rings had been flattened into dust-choked ruins. Watchtowers stood split open like hollowed trees, their courtyards choked with rubble. Buildings leaned at precarious angles, saved from total collapse only by the exposed Kuname beams that groaned under the strain. The royal messengers rode around the jagged boreholes drilled by the subterranean automaton rigs. They leapt over the mechanical carcasses of clockwork beasts and animal remains, reaching the collapsed homes of folks who survived the attack.

Alabi watched the recovery from the balcony of Chief Irabor's manor. Below, the people were already purging the wreckage, piling up rubble into horse-drawn carts, patching breaches in the foundations, and filling holes in the ground. Even the children joined in, though they were frequently distracted, scavenging through the tangles of gears and copper wiring strewn across the ground.

Through the clamour of reconstruction, the strings of an

akpata began to hum. A middle-aged man sat amongst the ruins, his voice starting as a low, gravelly vibration before ascending into a sonorous crescendo that seemed to vibrate through the very stones. The melody was a tapestry of memory, weaving together the ancient glory of Benin with a fierce, quiet hope for the dawn.

A small airship dipped out of the amber sky, its landing struts hissing as it touched down in the courtyard.

"They're here!" Alabi cried, his voice breaking with a sudden, sharp joy. He flew down the stairs, dashing through the hallways and past the infirmary where Ruka and Uche sat weary and slumped, their wounds being tended to by a healer.

Alabi stumbled out into the sunlight, adrenaline surging anew as Fara emerged from behind Uwa. She stepped onto the grass with a hesitant grace as if she feared it might vanish beneath her feet. Her eyes locked onto Alabi's. For a heartbeat, the world stood completely still. And then, with a cry of pure relief and joy, she ran. And jumped.

Alabi staggered backwards as he caught her in his arms as if she were the only thing left in the world that truly mattered. She wrapped her spindly legs around him, burying her face against the crook of his neck. Alabi could feel the viscous tension drain from her small frame. For the first time in her short, turbulent life, the world didn't feel like a succession of gears and pistons ready to crush her; she finally felt safe.

"Thank you," Alabi said, his voice thick with emotion as he looked up at Uwa.

Uwa met his gaze with a solemn, knowing nod, his expression etched with the weariness of the journey. He invoked the names of the lost like a sacred oath finally fulfilled.

"For Adesua and Imade."

The Queen Mother's cell, a monolithic cage forged from reinforced Kuname, was guarded day and night by the empire's most elite sentries. Benin's foremost inventors visited the prison under Isoken's unblinking eye, drawn to the deposed monarch like moths to a flame. Their conversations drifted across the vast landscape of the human condition—from the cold calculations of science and engineering to the philosophic extremes of slavery and power—always lasting deep into the night.

"She's dangerously well-read," Isoken reported during a private council with Ruka, Uche, Chief Irabor, and Alabi. "Speak with her long enough and her logic begins to feel frighteningly seductive. You could almost find yourself endorsing her beliefs."

The General paced the length of the room, her boots echoing on the polished floor. "Her real name is Merritt, daughter of Kianga, a native of East Africa. She revealed that her mother was an enslaved woman serving in England when she was assaulted by her captor. Merritt grew up in the smothering shadow of the Wilson manor, never knowing her father, a slave in all but name. When she was only eight, her mother was torn apart by hounds while shielding Merritt from their fury. It was only after this horror that a wealthy, childless widow adopted her, granting her access to a world of forbidden wealth and radical education."

"And the automaton army?" Uche asked, his brow furrowed.

"It was a relic," Isoken replied. "An abandoned research project she salvaged from the archives of her benefactors, which she then revived and redesigned into the nightmare that stood before our gates."

"Did she explain how she commands a legion with a single thought?" Irabor asked, leaning forward.

"No," Isoken said, her voice dropping. "She remains defiant. She insists that she is merely a precursor—that another will rise to take her place in the great gear-work of history."

Alabi shifted in his seat, his voice barely a whisper. "Did she say anything about my father?"

"Nothing," Isoken said, her voice and visage softening as she looked at Alabi. "Merritt views her subordinates as mere disposable components—pawns in a twisted quest for absolute dominion. The silver lining, Alabi, is that your father has been remarkably forthcoming."

Alabi's eyes widened, hopeful.

"Korede is providing the Guild with schematics and system overrides we never could have decoded on our own. Because of his cooperation, the Palace Court is considering a significant reduction of his sentence."

Alabi's heart raced, a tumult of relief and lingering grief crashing against his ribs. He had been forbidden from visiting the holding cells since the smoke had cleared, and the distance felt like a physical ache. Ruka, sensing the sudden tremor in his posture, reached out and anchored his hand with her own.

"Let us revel in this hard-won victory, my friends," Chief Irabor announced, his voice booming as he motioned to servants to bring forth gourds of frothing palm wine. "We were besieged, yet we conquered. We shall rise from these ruins more formidable than the legends of old. The Royal Court will soon formalise its gratitude for your extraordinary bravery and sacrifice," Irabor added, a rare, genuine smile creasing his weathered face. "And as a mark of supreme honour, you shall be granted an audience with the Great and Mighty One who walks where spirits walk—the Oba of Benin himself."

10

AUGUST, 2, 1866
BENIN EMPIRE, EDO-DELTA REGION

The throne room was thick with the scent of incense and the weight of centuries.

Armoured soldiers stationed themselves like iron pillars at opposite ends of the throne room chamber, each positioned beside the twelve bronze statues of the ancestral kings of Benin—silent, metallic witnesses and lineage holders for the living. Sunlight cascaded through the expansive windows, illuminating the marble floors where a massive symbol of the Great Bronze Mask was etched into the stone. The craftsmanship was so precise, the rendering so lifelike, that the mask appeared to be suspended within a luminous pool of art.

The Queen Mother stood at the centre of this theatre of justice, guarded by Isoken and a formidable platoon of sentries. Alabi, Ruka, and Uche stood together, watching this testament to their victory. They were flanked by Chief Irabor and the four high chiefs who sat in a semi-circle around the sovereign seat.

The Oba of Benin sat in imperial stillness, clad in a robe

of deep velvet crimson. His crown, a masterpiece of intricate coral and clay beads, shimmered under the light and he held a pristine white horsetail—the fly-whisk of divine authority—in his hand.

"The Queen Mother has been charged with the highest crimes against the Benin Kingdom: for crimes against humanity and for the calculated attempt to overthrow the Oba through acts of war and subjugation," Chief Irabor announced, the only chief standing. His pronouncement resonated against the vaulted ceiling. "She stands accused of the heresy of self-deification, proclaiming herself a god, several acts of terrorism, and the ruthless exploitation of the people. She is further charged with the barbarous mechanisation of slavery and cold-blooded murder, to name but a few of her sins."

Irabor scanned the room, his gaze resting momentarily on the prisoner. "The council has deliberated on two potential fates: a life of perpetual confinement, or the finality of execution. All those in favour of the sentence of death, signify now."

Every chief raised their hands, their expressions grim and unyielding.

The Oba flicked his horsetail—a deliberate, regal gesture of irrevocability—signifying his accord with the council's judgement. Immediately, Isoken and her sentries closed in, escorting the former Queen Mother from the throne room. As she was led away, the clatter of her brass shackles against the marble was the only sound in the vast chamber, a mechanical dirge for a fallen empire.

"We hope to extract every fragment of intelligence she possesses before the execution," Chief Irabor declared, his clear voice resounding with authority. "We have sent word to every village and city-state previously crushed under her heel. We have announced the Queen Mother's fall, and the resistance no longer lingers in the shadows. They march with a fierce boldness as the peoples' vanguard, dismantling the scorched remnants of her reign. The automatons have been deactivated; their central command-lattice was shattered, ending the conflict and the oppression throughout the regions. Merritt still warns of shadows yet to rise—of disciples who share her cold vision—but let them come. We will be ready. The Empire of Benin shall emerge from this fire more formidable than it has ever been."

The gathered chiefs nodded, their coral clay beads clinking in a rhythmic chorus of agreement.

"And what of the architect?" one of the chiefs asked, casting a sharp, sidelong glance toward Alabi. "The man who forged the giants and the instruments of our destruction?"

"The inventor provided the warning that saved our city from becoming a tomb, and for that, we owe him our lives," Irabor stated firmly. "He will serve a ten-year term of confinement, during which his expertise on the inner workings of the clockwork legions will be utilised by our Guild. We believe his mind is a resource we cannot afford to lose."

Irabor briefly locked eyes with Alabi. The young man heaved a staggering sigh of relief, as the crushing weight of anxiety lifted.

"To the ones who cast themselves into the fire to save the empire—Ruka, Uche, and Alabi," Irabor said, turning to face them fully. "We officially recognise you as Exalted Allies of our kingdoms. You three have demonstrated a degree of bravery and selflessness that borders on the legendary. You shall be rewarded with estates and titles befitting your sacrifice…"

Alabi caught Irabor's eye and gave a subtle, meaningful signal. The Chief paused, reading the silent request in the boy's gaze, and gave a slow, respectful nod of understanding.

With a profound bow, Irabor spoke, his voice carrying through the hallowed air. "Alabi of Itu Agan—the man who warned us of the impending attack, the man who cast himself into the path of destruction to preserve this city—wishes to petition the Crown."

The chiefs exchanged searching glances, and the Oba of Benin gave a slow, deliberate wave of his horsetail in agreement. Alabi took a deep, steadying breath.

"Mighty king," he began, his voice gaining strength as he spoke. "Esteemed Chiefs. I recognise that the Kingdom of Benin is the cradle of our civilisation, a sanctuary for the greatest craftsmen, inventors, and warriors in all the land.

I understand your desire to shield this history, to remain a sacred island apart from the world. But these years of blood have proven that isolation is a slow death. We must be united. The people beyond these walls are being crushed by colonists; they need weapons forged of your unbreakable alloy and spirits forged by your example."

He looked at the council, his eyes burning with desperate sincerity. "Some of my kin have known only the shackles of slavery. They have forgotten the spirit of resistance. We need the Benin people to lend them your fire, to show them that we can rebel—and win—against tyranny, and most importantly of all: to give them hope."

A murmur rippled through the chiefs like a coming storm.

"Are you asking us to open up our walls?" one chief asked, his voice sharp with suspicion.

"No, fair Chief," Alabi countered firmly. "I'm asking you to share the light of your knowledge. I am asking you to lend your technology and your steel, and intervene when our nation falls under siege. Let us destroy our enemies at the shore, before they can ever hope to extinguish our freedom."

"All in favour of declining the petition, signify now," Chief Irabor said. Three hands rose into the air, as solid and unmoving as the bronze statues surrounding them. Alabi felt his stomach twist into a cold, hard knot, but he resolved to keep it together.

"Those in favour of accepting the petition?"

Chief Irabor and one other raised their hands. Alabi's shoulders slouched, the weight of a failed future pressing down on him. But then, the Oba of Benin leaned forward. He made a subtle signal to the chief nearest him, a whisper that sparked through the council until the murmuring fell into a reverent silence.

"The Oba of Benin," Irabor announced, his voice ringing with the weight of history, "accepts your petition. The gates of knowledge shall be opened."

Alabi sank to his knees, the marble floor cold against his skin—yet his heart was ablaze with gratitude. "Thank you!"

Alabi sat in the undulating golden tall grass of the lush savannah, watching the last surviving herd of ostriches from afar. He drank in the stark beauty of the horizon—the pristine ribbon of the stream and the emerald leaves of acacias swaying under the wind's rhythmic touch—while his thoughts remained anchored to his father in his bleak stone cell.

The past few days had been a gauntlet of emotional extremes. He was navigating the aching loss of his mother alongside the bitter reality of his father's imprisonment.

There were, of course, radiant silver linings that kept him from sinking—mitigating the bombs and convincing the Benin Empire to share their knowledge with the outside world.

There was also the memory of Ruka's kiss and the fresh glint of admiration in her eyes whenever her gaze met his. Being with her made him sink into a world of blissful imagination where his life was not a series of broken parts, but a completed masterpiece. He found himself wishing she had known his mother; he imagined them in the savannah, their voices twining in laughter as they pointed at the ostriches, giggling and sharing the quiet, resilient gossip about the woes of womanhood.

The reality, however, was far colder. Alabi had carried the news of his mother's passing to the dungeon, and had watched his father crumble like a pillar of salt doused in a tempest. Korede's tears flowed freely without shame. "Please, tell me it's a lie," he begged through agonising sobs. Alabi wished for the same—that the blood on his hands and the smoke in his lungs had been nothing more than a fever-dream.

"It's true," Alabi had said, his voice a steady, mournful chime. "She's gone, Bàámì."

Korede's gaze had lingered on him then, his eyes clouded with a slow, aching recognition of the colossal weight his son had carried in his absence. Alabi had grown accustomed to the painful density in his chest, a gravity that he knew he would never truly escape. He required no pity, least of all from the man who had built the machines of their undoing. He had extended his arm through the cold iron railings in a gesture of comfort, but Korede could not bring himself to touch it.

His father's shock had fractured into raw hysteria, a cacophony of wailing and grinding of teeth at the unberable magnitude of his loss. He had curled into a pitiful ball, shrinking away from the light until his head was tucked in between his knees, a broken man in a bronze cage.

"My Labake," he sobbed, the name a shattered prayer. "My sweet, sweet Labake."

"Alabi!" Ruka called through the golden stillness, her voice cutting through his thoughts, bright and sharp.

She reached him with a beaming, breathless smile, her eyes dancing with a fire he had never seen before. "Isoken has promised to mentor me! She's taking me into the vanguard!" She laughed, a sound like clear water over stone. "And guess what? Uncle Uche approves. He finally looked at me, Alabi—truly looked at me—and acknowledged the path I've chosen."

Ruka's joy was visceral and contagious, an electric current that pulled Alabi from the depths of his own mourning. Looking at her, he felt a sudden, fierce desire to shed his sorrow and simply bathe in her light.

"I'm so proud of you, Ruka," he said, his voice thick with sincerity. "Your mother would have been awed by the woman you've become."

Tears shimmered in her eyes as she pulled him into a fierce embrace. The scent of crushed grass and rain clung to her clothes. "I'm certain your mother is watching with the same pride. Enough now. Stop brooding. Come with me."

She reached down and entwined her fingers with his, her grip firm and warm. She pulled him upward, leading him away from his grief, away from the weight of the dungeon and the shadows of his worries, and into a secluded sanctuary where no one could follow.

EPILOGUE

AUGUST, 2, 1883
BENIN EMPIRE, EDO-DELTA REGION

The grating screech of the dungeon gates echoed through the courtyard, and Korede stepped into the world, squinting at the blinding afternoon light. He had become a man of sharp angles; his frame had grown lean, and the wrinkles around his eyes had deepened into permanent furrows of regret.

Alabi stood waiting for him beside a horse-drawn cart. He caught his father's cursory, searching glances and knew exactly what the man was looking for: the ghost of the son he had left behind. But that boy was gone. In his place stood a man whose shoulders were broad enough to carry the weight of an empire, his hands calloused not just by tools, but by the grit of survival.

Korede opened his mouth to speak, but the words were lost when Alabi surged forward, scooping his father into a tight embrace. There, amidst the gleaming light breaking through the palace grounds, they both wept—a violent, necessary release. Finally, Alabi pulled away, his expression a mix of mercy and strength, and helped his father into the cart.

"There's something I want to show you, Bààmì," he said, quiet, hard-earned pride ringing in his voice.

The horses galloped toward the Great Benin Lake, where the vast, blue sky was perfectly mirrored on the glassy surface. On the shore, Alabi led him toward a shape sitting proudly against the reeds by the shores of the lake. Tears of pure wonder streamed down Korede's face as he sighted a sleek, bronze-plated steamboat.

"I built it myself," Alabi said, his hand resting on the warm, polished hull. "For the longest time, I lived in the shadow of your genius, fearing I could never be the inventor you were. But these past years, I have been privileged enough to find my own fire—to challenge the metal until it bends to my will."

Korede gazed at the craft, his fingers trembling as he traced the flawless welding and the elegant curve of the steam chimney.

"It's beautiful, Alabi," he whispered, his voice thick with awe. "It is a masterpiece."

Alabi's eyes crinkled with a smile. "Come on, Bààmì," Alabi said, his arm anchoring the man whose shadow he had once chased along the banks of Itu Agan. A steady hand for a fading giant. "There are many more things I wish to show you."

THE END.

ACKNOWLEDGEMENTS

I am proud to have written this African Steampunk novella as it is the first of its kind and, hopefully, the first of many.

To my esteemed alpha and beta readers Uchechukwu Nwaka, Plangdi Neple, Damilola Oyedotun, Amadin Ogbewe, Olayinka Yakub, Jacky Days Otto, Andrew Keahey, and Chinedu Herbert—thank you for your insightful comments and for believing in the greatness that is this book. To the wonderful writers of Milford Science Fiction Writers Workshop 2024 and the AbsoluteWrite "Share Your Story" forum, many thanks for the detailed review of my manuscript.

To my publisher, R. B. Wood, who believes in my predestined success, thank you for recognizing my artistry and granting me the opportunity to share it with the world. Deborah Brannon and Steve Pamplin, my deepest gratitude for your dedication, enthusiasm, and attention to detail.

None of this would've been possible without my family's support. To my mom and dad, Adejoke and Thompson Eselojor, thank you for birthing me, for your continuous encouragement and support, and for exposing me to my

Edo and Yoruba heritage. Because of you, our culture and our legacy shines through these pages. To my brother, Promise Eselojor, who has been supportive of my dreams my entire life, thank you for never wavering and for being the epitome of brotherly love. To my other siblings, Sandra and Daniel Eselojor, who boast of my intelligence and perceived riches, thank you for adding colour to my life.

To the friends and wonderful folks who have cheered for me from the beginning, who noticed my spark before I began to burn brightly, I see you, and I adore you. May you be honoured in the same manner.

And to my beloved sky daddy, who I would speak to under the guise of talking to myself, thank you for making my brain so magnificent.

ABOUT NAOMI ESELOJOR

Naomi Eselojor is a speculative fiction writer from Nigeria and a global talent migrant endorsed by the Arts Council England for her contributions to Africanfuturism. She is the recipient of the 2023 Utopian Award for Short Fiction and the 2024 Wilson Okereke Prize for Short Stories, and has also been a finalist for the Nommo Award as well as nominated for the Pushcart Prize, Ako Caine Prize, and Utopian Awards. Naomi's works have appeared in *Afrofuturism Short Stories, African Ghost Short Stories, 2022 Best of Utopian Speculative Fiction, Omenana Magazine, Lolwe, Hexagon Magazine, Dark Matter Magazine,* and elsewhere. Among other programs, Naomi is an alum of Milford Writer's Workshop, the Voodoonauts Fellowship, and served as a Sprinng mentor in 2024 and 2025. Most recently, she was selected to run a workship with the London Writers Centre's Developing Tutors 2025/2026 season. She resides in the United Kingdom.

ALSO BY NAOMI ESELOJOR

"Neyllo," published in *Omenana,* Issue 22, and reprinted in *2022 Best of Utopian Speculative Fiction* by Android Press. (Winner of the Utopian Award for short fiction, 2023)

"My Mother's Love," published in *Hexagon SF Magazine,* Issue 10, and reprinted in *African Ghost Short Stories* by Flame Tree Press, 2023. (Shortlisted for the 2024 Nommo Award and reviewed by Alex Brown in "Must-Read Speculative Short Fiction for September 2022" in *Reactor* magazine)

"Enitan," published in *Lolwe,* Issue 6, 2022. (Nominated for the AKO Caine Prize for African Writing)

"Krest," published in the *Things Improbable* anthology by Improbable Press, 2023.

"The Black Bird," published in *Akéwì Magazine,* 2023.

"The Seventy-Year-Old Corpse Harvester," published in *Dark Matter Magazine,* 2023, and reprinted in *Afrofuturism Short Stories* by Flame Tree Press.

being pulled into a beautifully vivid, alternate 19th-century world where clockwork and culture mix. The narrative handles massive themes of colonial subjugation and family fracturing with a surprising gentleness and intimacy that keeps you rooted in Alabi's perspective."

—**Somto Ihezue**, Nebula finalist and Locus Award-winning author of *We Begin Where Infinity Ends*

"*The City of Factories* is a powerful debut, set in a richly crafted world that is as gripping as it is moving. Eselojor's deft storytelling draws you in and makes it easy to root for the young inventor Alabi, desperate to find his father in a city run by an automaton army. Eselojor takes us on a thrilling ride as Alabi faces a shadowy resistance and a mysterious empire holding its cards close. There are plenty of surprises on the way, and lovers of dystopian steampunk will relish every step of the journey."

—**Cheryl S. Ntumy**, author of *They Made Us Blood and Fury*

"If you love Nnedi Okorafor and Naomi Novik, you need to read this book. With *The City of Factories*, Eselojor puts forth an impressive debut indeed, a powerful steampunk fairy tale that examines colonialism, cultural conflict, and complicity. Ultimately a resistance tale, this novella emphasizes empathy, showing that even a small kindness can be an act of revolution. Once I picked it up, it was incredibly hard to put down. This book is electric."

—**Kemi Ashing-Giwa**, scientist and *USA Today* bestselling author of *The Splinter in the Sky*

PRAISE FOR THE CITY OF FACTORIES

"Eselojor's vivid transformation of Apapa into a cacophonous city of factories is enthralling while attentive to the colonial history that bore the real city. If you're looking for Afrocentric steampunk with earnest and scrappy heroes, in the tradition of Tobi Ogundiran and P. Djélì Clark by way of *Arcane*, you'll find it here."

— **Suyi Davies Okungbowa**, award-winning author of *Lost Ark Dreaming* and The Nameless Republic trilogy

"Written with a sure voice and masterful pacing, Eselojor's story of young Alabi seeking to rescue his father from the clutches of oppression highlights the painful and sometimes doomed choices one must make in the face of tyranny. A riveting story from a writer to watch!"

— **Tobi Ogundiran**, British Fantasy and Ignyte Award-winning author of the Guardians of the Gods series

"*The City of Factories* is a soulful steampunk tale of automation and industrialism, mortality and the cost of our decisions, the search for family, challenging binaries and biases, and resistance."

— **Ai Jiang**, Ignyte, Bram Stoker, and Nebula Award-winning author of *Linghun*

"*The City of Factories* is a complex father-son relationship and coming-of-age story ensconced in a larger tale of oppression, resistance, and reclamation. It feels like